The Lake of Love

Also by Che Chidi Chukwumerije:

Prose
Twice is not enough
There is always something more

Poetry
Palm Lines
The Beautiful Ones have been born
Writing is the Happiness of Sorrow
Light of Awakening
River
Cumbrian Lines: Poems born of the Lake District
Innengart (*poems in german*)
Das dauerhafte Gedicht (*poems in german*)
Mmiri a zoro nwayọ nwayọ (*poems in igbo*)

For children
Somayinozo's Stories

Che Chidi Chukwumerije – The Lake of Love.
Second Edition 2015
First Edition 2012 under the pseudonym Aka Teraka.
Boxwood Publishing House e.K.
Copyright © Che Chidi Chukwumerije 2012.
All rights reserved.
ISBN 978-3-943000-80-1

Cover Photo: Lake Grasmere © Yvonne Chukwumerije

Che Chidi Chukwumerije

THE LAKE OF LOVE

a philosophical journey

...

Boxwood Publishing House, Frankfurt

Table of Contents

Forward

. . .

THE SEARCH for God is the most powerful, irresistible, the driving, force within the destiny of every individual. God as a Concept or God as a Person. God within the name 'GOD' or within the activity 'LIFE'. God far, God near. God as the Beginning of Religion or as the End of Science.

The search takes many forms, bears many names, reaches many conclusions. It does not end. Whether mankind knows it or not, forgets or remembers it, acknowledges or contests it, it has driven them through all the milestones that unitedly form the History of the human race. And whereas the one seeks the Godhead in order to serve It, the other seeks God with the hope of becoming It.

It is convenient to stop at the usual imagery called up by the well-known word 'GOD', bury the matter there and return to one's life. But that exactly is the point. That life to which one returns is the perpetual search for the whole point. Religion exists, science exists, conflict exists, development exists, the hunger for more exists because everything that bears life or motion within itself seems to be locked in an unending struggle to unlock the very essence of the source of that very life.

Concepts come alive within us which we strive to realise in deed. That is the beginning and the end of our story.

This story is set simply in the landscape of the author's mind, detached from accepted time and space. Concepts arise like trees, mountains, that crumble to be blown away like the shifting sands of transient or bridge-ideologies. Thoughts are birds, or streams, into which the restless net is cast, story caught, holding on like lightning to an immortal's trident, a man's mind.

The concept: There was once a man called Scimarajh, an ordinary man living in the midst of other human beings. He did what everybody else did. Maybe he learned a trade, built a house, married a wife, raised children. He probably engaged himself in his community and occasionally met with his friends for a drink. If there were any other thoughts in his head than those connected to these activities, he kept them to himself.

One day, he heard about a faraway place called the Land of Bliss. A place where, it was said, he would find himself and thereby experience joy. And for the first time in his life, Scimarajh admitted to his wife, his family, his friends and his community that he was unhappy...

And he set out to find the Land of Bliss. At the point in time at which we encounter him, he has already faced and overcome the mightiest of tests that lay upon his path in his journey. And now, only one small obstacle, unexpected by him, remains. A little lake that would stand, impassable, in his way. A lake called Love by the beings who live in this strange valley.

Che Chidi Chukwumerije

i.

The Face In The Tears

...

Che Chidi Chukwumerije

...

SCIMARAJH – THE seeker and the humble – had already *crossed seven Deserts, sailed seven Seas and sojourned seven Forests in his journey towards the Land of Bliss.* –

Now he stood just a few moments away from arriving the towering gate of Bliss-land.

Calmly he stood atop a little plateau and gazed back at the vast distances and adventures he had overcome to attain to this point. As his physical eyes roamed the horizon, and his mental eyes his adventures all over again, the eyes of his spirit beheld in gratitude and silence the lessons that he had gained from his experiences.

Today he was quite a humbled one.

Finally his soul quietened and he slowly turned around to face the direction in which he still had to go; as he turned, the four winds seemed to turn with him, and accompanied his questing, yearning gaze towards the east, towards the country of the rising sun, the Land of Bliss.

There it was, swathed in a warm, rosy glow and sending forth sounds like the sweet tinkling of tiny bells. Above the Land was an immense rainbow, and just above the rainbow hovered a new bird, small as a crescent moon, yet radiating with such all-powerful intensity that it compelled the beholding eye to quickly look away lest it be dazzled too brightly, and filled the heart almost to the point of bursting!

The Land of Bliss...

Like the sweet fragrance of a blossomed flower, bliss enveloped the soul of Scimarajh as he gazed in steadfast longing towards the high, luminous walls, studded with a silver-white gate, which enclosed the longed-for Land.

The Land of Bliss. Object of the longing of so many human souls, crowning of the journey of every man ... and here he stood, Scimarajh, gazing at it. Why? Was he truly worth it?

Scimarajh bent his head and sent up a humble prayer of unending gratitude to GOD, Lord of all Creations! Nature grew silent with his prayer, and a ray of light descended like an unending arrow into the humble soul of Scimarajh. He straightened as the liquid fire of Divine Love raced through every nerve, every vein, every corridor of his entire being.

Then he looked up. His eyes had changed. They had become deeper, more intense, a soft glow emanated therefrom. He now had but one desire – to climb the hill in front of him on top of which magnificently arose the Land of Bliss.

He took one last look across from the plateau on which he stood, to the top of the crystal giant-hill on the other side, at the end of his journey. The end gave him power to start off afresh and for the last time towards it...

Scimarajh gathered his garments firmly about him, tested his back-pack slung over his shoulder, and began to quickly descend the high-ground, into the valley.

As he descended the plateau, he exalted in nature. He saw the azure-blue skies stretching protectively above his head, and around him he saw beauty unveiled. The green of the grass was of a tone he had never before quite seen. It seemed to have a restorative effect on him. The flowers were beautiful. Multicoloured, as if a rainbow had exploded in the skies and the little splittings of colour had showered themselves upon the fields. Was this real? He thought back to the world of men. Had he ever seen anything so beautiful? No. Not ever. Not once.

He strolled through these fields briskly. Much as they delighted his eyes and watered the garden that was his soul, he could tarry not even for a single second. His eyes were focused yet detached. Paradise was still in front.

And then there was a lake...

As he approached the valley …. suddenly and for the first time, he noticed *a lake* that nestled right in the heart of the greens, stretching wide into the woods on either side, but perhaps only about forty or sixty strides across. He hesitated for one second, his eyebrows lifted. He had *not* seen the lake from the top of the plateau.. He had not been looking into the valley, but only up at the Land of Bliss.

But only for a moment did he hesitate. His strides picked up speed and certainty once more and he headed straight for the lake. After crossing seven seas, amongst other things, a little lake was not going to bother him in any way now that he was so close to the Land.

As he neared the lake, it suddenly dawned on him that nature seemed to have changed. It appeared to have come alive. Suddenly the grass was whispering, but whispering *what?* He could tell not. The leaves were talking, but talking to whom – to him, or simply to themselves? The wind sang a song, a wordless song, and from the sides of his eyes he thought he could catch the flashy movements of little things. *Almost like little human beings.* Little human-like beings? He swung his head sharply on all sides…nothing. Only the green, beautifully decorated fields. The enchanting woods.

In him something began to stir. He knew that there was a discussion going on in nature, a conversation, an exchange of opinions...or, wait, a message?

Again Scimarajh hesitated. He wanted to find out what was going on around him. Or, rather, a part of him wanted to – the curious part...or, is it, the *cautious* part? But the larger part of him, the adventurer who had surmounted high and low, the seeker who had journeyed tirelessly, was impatient.

Move on! The command thundered forcefully within him, borne of a long–persevering hunger, a long-unfulfilled desire. So he tore his attention away from the mysterious, imperceptible activity going on around him and quickly took the last brisk strides that brought him to the edge of the lake.

The lake was silent. Motionless. Clear as the surface of a perfectly-polished mirror. Still.

Scimarajh gazed at it, equally silent, equally still. His mind ticked. A deep seriousness, immense and grave, settled over his beautiful countenance.

There was something about this lake on which he could not place his finger. Something mysterious. Something as yet unfathomed. Unravelled. And yet, why did he get the impression that he had seen this lake before? He looked at the lake and the lake looked back at him with his own eyes, his own face, his own self. Who knows himself? Scimarajh?

But other thoughts than these occupied him. How deep was the lake? How safe? He was not deceived by the apparent calm of the lake. The last months and years of his life had brought him danger in all forms, at unexpected turns, and he had learned to take nothing for granted. Not even a little lake.

He looked about. Nature's voice had increased in volume. So Scimarajh calmed down. By his feet lay a long, thin pole. He picked it up and, holding it at one end, slowly immersed it into the water of the lake. Nothing. Presently he revolved his hand, stirring the water and all the while peering pin-point sharp into it, tense and concentrated.

After a long time of testing and watching, investigating, checking and waiting, his body slowly relaxed; the skin around his eyes, formerly tightened, smoothened out again and he let the faithful pole back out of the lake, carefully replacing it back down by his feet where it had formerly lain.

The lake was safe, just like any other.

Now that he had become satisfied of that, his movements again became brisk and sure. Speedily he took off his garments, knelt down in the soft, mossy grass and folded them. Then he opened up his little back-pack and gazed with delighted eyes at its contents.

Three beautiful precious stones, his sole possessions and objects of his deep love. He had acquired them laboriously through his long, long journeys. And he guarded them with all his might, for without them he would never make his way into the Land of

Bliss. His former teacher, the Master of the Sea, had told him so himself. And he was going to present them to the King of Joy when he finally made his entry into the Land of Bliss.

He could not suppress the cry of joy that escaped his lips as his heart soared in these thoughts. Then he came back to the moment. To work! To work! Quickly, but very neatly, he folded his faithful garments one more time and arranged them inside the back-pack. Then, arising anew, he strapped the pack unto his back and prepared to dive in. He concentrated.

Suddenly he heard it. Loud and clear!

A voice.

"Do not dive into the Lake of Love!" –

Scimarajh started up, whipped his head around, saw nobody. He looked and looked. Nothing stirred. Nature had quietened again. Had he heard wrong? He listened hard and heard absolute silence communing with itself.

The silence filled him like a wave.

His head began to swim. Not for a second did it occur to him to immerse himself in the feeling. To know what it was. Rather he resisted it. *What?*, he thought. *After getting so close?! ... No way! ...*

He shook his head vigorously and sharpened his eyes on the silver-surface of the lake. *I must have heard wrong*, he told himself repeatedly, remembering the mirages he once used to see in the deserts and the imaginary sounds he once also heard in the forests when tension was high. *It must be the same phenomenon,* he assured himself, *and the nearness of the end of my journey is making me dizzy.*

In his heart of hearts, however, a contrary intuition stirred, but he drowned it with the clamour of his thoughts, and his desire.

Bent at the knee ... tensed his muscles ... breathed in ... and dived in ... - straight as a spear and just as sharp.

He cut the surface of the water silently, barely causing a ripple, and made absolute sure that he did not in any measure go too deeply below the surface. He levelled up straight-away and began to swim across the lake, gliding smoothly in ephemerally beautiful strokes, his body fit, his yearning drawing him forward like a returning rubber-band.

He swam at a measured pace, not too slowly, not too fast. The water was cool, cool and yet, in a strange way, very warm. It seemed to grip him like a gentle hug and assist him in his swim.

Something in him relaxed. He *had* been hearing unreal voices; the water was safe.

Towards the middle of the lake, he pushed his head fully under the water for the first time and peered in. Crystal-clear green and very transparent. He saw straight down to the bottom. It was a shallow lake. Clear she was. No fishes. No insects. No movements. And at the bottom it was simply dark soil.

What was it that had made him hesitant to dive in, then? Suddenly his curiosity was aroused. There was something magnetic about that still, dark soil at the bottom of the lake. It seemed to be saying: *Come to me, wanderer, come to me ... I hold a treasure, a treasure, a treasure...*

And Scimarajh yielded. One last extraction of his head, a deep intake of air, and with a quick flip he was piking downwards towards the bottom. Why? He did not know really. Just to stand on it. To feel it. To know.

And then – without warning – it hit him, the *strange* chill, piercing into his very blood like a knife-stab, and with it a force beyond compare seemed to have arisen from all sides, and it gripped him but in-detachably!

Like quick-silver, he did a sharp flip and faced the surface again, the bright surface aglow with the radiance of the sun beaming down upon it.

And he began to struggle, to struggle like he had never struggled in his life before – not when he rode across the deserts or sailed the seven wild seas or battled through the seven hideous forests.

This one was different. An unholy dread gripped his heart, dread the sort of which no other situation of danger had awakened in him; he would for long never know what saved him. Or, perhaps, who.

Nor how he surged upwards again out of that strange, ice cold region that gripped him with elemental force and made his head dizzy.

He shot to the surface, as frightened as a hare. Once there, he took just one moment to note the side of the lake on which the Land of Bliss stood and then he powered thitherto, *a wanderer shaken*!

The opposite bank arrived his fingers and he quickly hoisted himself out of the clear, silver-screen lake, dripping with water and fear, gasping, at once shivering and sweating.

Seconds became minutes and more minutes and then, finally and slowly, he returned to normal.

But he remained sitted on the grass by the lake, making sure there was a safer distance between them, and let his body stabilise itself completely through the taking of deep, slow breaths.

As he did this he, almost hesitantly (for thus great had his fear been), began to reflect on the nature of the strange, frightening force at work deeper within the heart of this lake. It had been so frightening.

Was that why nature had tried to warn him? Suddenly he no longer regarded the disembodied voice he'd heard on the other side of the lake as being imaginary – it had been real! Again, gratitude awakened in his soul for who- or whatever it was that had issued the warning. Nature seemed to reply with a sudden deepening of colour and then becoming normal again.

And he, Scimarajh, wanderer, stranger to men, dreamer and seeker of truth who normally understood the unobtrusive voice of nature, for the second time within so short a while failed to grasp nature's word to him. He only felt an unfamiliar vibration waft over to him, hover there for but moments and then was all too quickly gone.

His body had recovered. And immediately his venture's call surged into him again. His goal! The Land of Bliss ... of Bliss, oh Bliss ... he was so tired. He could not wait any longer for his rest. Finally, after *all* that through which he had been, he needed the rest.

Up. He sprang up! Time to go up the hill... – *but*...

Irony of ironies....! Involuntarily a pained cry escaped his terror-stricken face. Because only for the first time since he had come out of the lake, he realised... *that his back-pack was gone!* Gone. Gone *into the heart, down to the bottom, of the lake.*

And standing there, staring helplessly towards the clear surface of the lake, Scimarajh sank slowly down to his knees and began to weep.

In the struggle against the uncanny force inside the lake, his back-pack must have somehow gotten torn off his back and sank dead straight to the dark, murky bottom with all his possessions – his lovingly woven and cared-for garments and his three precious, precious, precious stones. Tools for his entry into the Land of Bliss, each one given to him by an act of fate along his path. Ha had been warned to guard them with all his Heart, for without them he would never find his way into the Land of Bliss. And now they were gone. *Why had he not felt it happen!*

His head hung down like a folded wing, and his tears slowly, one by one, each one making its movement felt, slid down his cheeks and dropped unto the green grass like iridescent crystals. They were tears of remorse. He had been warned.

He had no-one to blame but himself. Only himself. His foolish, self-willed, sad self. Minutes went by and Scimarajh was still kneeling by the Lake of Love, weeping, clad in but his simple, body-clogging inner cloth and in his pain, a human heart in anguish...

Years upon years of seeking. *All* in vain. Like dry wood, his heart splintered, broke, cracked ... and he gazed upon the image of his tortured soul. Suddenly it seemed to him that his entire journey had been but a futile waste of time, ending in nothingness.

As he wept so heart-searingly, consumed by his unbearable anguish, unnoticed by him his tears were percolating into a little pool there on the ground, a pool of tears, as clear as the lake and just as still, too, except for the dropping in of more tears, widening and enriching this little pool of tears. As if by magic, the tears did not drain away, but just pooled there beneath his sad countenance.

But then finally even his melted heart dried out and the tears stopped falling, but he remained motionless in his position, trying to find the composure, *and excuse*, to pray!

And then he heard his name.

Clear. Distinct. From beneath his sorrowfully bowed head:

"Scimarajh."

Startled, he started and looked fitfully in the direction from which he had heard his name. What he saw was so shocking that he almost jumped back in alarm. It was only his present state of depression which held him in place. But his eyes widened, for there, right there in front of him, beneath him, was a *strange face*, smiling slightly, and looking him straight in the eye.

And it had simply, as if by magic, appeared there on the rich, gleaming surface of his pool of tears. So and truly shocked was Scimarajh that he could only utter:

"Yes?"

"Why are you crying, Scimarajh?" the face in his tears said in a voice that seemed unendingly rich in love. And the eyes, glowing softly like distant moons, seemed to emit a soft warmth that gently enveloped Scimarajh and comforted him. They seemed to be saying: *it's alright, son, it's alright*. And Scimarajh's heart-breaking anguish and deep sorrow departed from him like night with the advent of dawn. And he calmed down. And spoke. And said, simply:

"Who are you?"

The smiling face in Scimarajh's pool of tears smiled even more softly, broadly, calming the wanderer's soul.

"I," said the face, "am your helper."

Scimarajh was startled once more.

"My helper? – but how? I don't understand. I have a helper? Who made you - ...? When –" he stopped short, the movements in his soul too quick for his stammering tongue.

"Everybody has a helper," said the face. "Even I myself. And I am yours."

"But *I* am nobody's helper!" cried Scimarajh, confused, his back-pack and dilemma temporarily forgotten.

But his helper only smiled at that. And said:

"Finally we shall know..."

Scimarajh stared into this strange face, never before seen, which identified itself as his helper's. Everything was so strange here.

"Where are we? What kind of place is this?"

The strange face smiled and said:

"Oh, but Scimarajh, the moment you crossed that plateau you entered into the Kingdom of Honesty."

Scimarajh made a strange face.

"Kingdom of Honesty? What's that?"

"Here all growth and development is accelerated; and whilst here each person receives immediately the fruits of his thoughts and actions, without fail or delay. Only those who strive honestly can survive here. And at the heart of the Kingdom of Honesty is the Lake of Love…"

This was too much for Scimarajh. New experiences, new information, a new reality, all at once. And this strange person, strange *face*, talking to him as if it was the most natural thing in the world. And something else – his voice sounded familiar. *Where* had he heard that voice before?

"Since when," he asked, "have you been my helper?"

"Since the moment you stood at the other bank of the Lake of Love, about to dive in."

And then it clicked! Of course! This was the exact same voice that had told him not to dive into the Lake … *of Love*, he had called it.

For the second time *that name. Why?* But, first, something more pressing –

"It was you!" cried Scimarajh in newly-awakened anguish. "You it was who tried to stop me from diving blindly into the lake! Oh, if only I had listened!"

The helper said nothing, but kept silent.

Everything returned to Scimarajh – the pain and the loss.

"What am I going to do?" asked Scimarajh.

"What do you want to do?" responded his helper.

"Why, I want to retrieve my back-pack of course!"

His helper smiled.

"Why?"

Scimarajh gazed earnestly into the love-filled eyes of his helper; love-filled and yet, in a strange way, also *stern*.

"Seven seas have I sailed and seven deserts conquered and through seven thick forests have I bravely wandered, seeking my goal, the earnest desire of my soul, the Land of Bliss. I renounced the world, wiles and ways of men and, painful as it was, separated myself from my family.

"And through my journeys and in my sojourn, I've acquired new knowledge, new faith, new sight, and all my riches and wealth and fame traded I for one lovely garment and three precious stones of unmatched beauty.

"Only to get to this mysterious lake and, driven by impatience, rather than by patience, ignored your warning ... and now all my life's work is gone – the most beautiful garment of earthly material with which to step into the Land of Bliss, and the three most precious stones of all the changing worlds, the first for the King, the second for his Queen, and the third as a gift to the entire Kingdom.

"Oh what shall I do, helper, what shall I do? My

journey is in shambles, my life is in vain..."

Scimarajh ended on a note of entreaty, broken by his loss, his impatience, his pain; a man at the valley of his lonely life, a horse seeking pasture, a bird in a cage.

His helper gazed at him, the love in his eyes deeper that it ever had been.

"Scimarajh!" he called, and his voice trembled slightly.

"Aye?" responded the wanderer.

"You seek that bag that contains the fruits of your experiencing – all that you have and can give?"

"Aye," answered Scimarajh again, voice with hope a-tinged.

"And then, *what?*" enquired his helper.

"Eh - ?" Scimarajh was startled. He had not expected that, nor was he certain that he truly comprehended it.

"I don't understand your question, helper."

"When you have retrieved your bag, what do you intend to do thereupon?"

"Well...," began Scimarajh, unbalanced for some reason by this simple question. "First I would dry my garments if they have become wet. Definitely. Then I would let them stretch out and regain their beautiful sheen. And then I would polish the precious stones. Finally I would dress up and head happily with the gems for the Land of Bliss!" He stopped, not certain if there was more he ought to say but had not.

The helper said nothing but simply pierced Scima-rajh's eyes with the suddenly very stern look in his. He was no longer smiling. His face was grave.

"Is that *all*, Scimarajh?!" he finally spoke. Sharp.

Scimarajh's uncertainty grew. He could only just barely prevent himself from looking away from his helper's blazing gaze. Besides that, anyhow, those uncanny eyes seemed to be magnets now, holding Scimarajh fast.

Suddenly he had the impression that he had gazed into these self-same eyes a million times before, each time he was going astray. They had followed him, ad-monishing. But his helper said he had only come to him as he stood on the other side of the lake. Scima-rajh could not really understand, could not even re-ally think.

The helper's last question still hovered unending-ly in the morning-air.

Finally, Scimarajh, fidgeting like a scolded child, croaked in a low, guilt-laden voice – but guilty with what?

"Should there be anything more, sir?"

"Human soul!" Was this his helper talking? Sud-denly he had become so cold. And on went the voice:

"*How* do you intend to enter into the Land of Bliss when you get to the Shinning Gate?"

"How? ... I know that not, oh hel- "

"Do you not know that, aeons ago, as you exited the Land of Bliss, unconscious, as a seed, to you was given the key of the Gate of the Bliss-Land?"

"To me?" cried Scimarajh.

"To *every human soul*!" announced his helper slowly. "Now," continued he, "*Where* have you placed your key, human?!"

There was something about the question. It seemed to tug at hidden strings, at the ends of which hung heavy but sensitive memories. He tried to find the emotional strength to pull up these inchoate memories. But the strings were too thin, hard to grasp, and the stirrings of memory, heavy-laden, continued to weigh at the dark bottom of a half-resurrected psyche. For the first time ever in his life, Scimarajh fell truly and completely *silent*. Empty as a vacuum. Nothing. It seemed to him that he had lost something of even more value than he could have ever guessed before. Frozen inside, he stared at the gap in his understanding.

How long he remained so, death-like silent and empty, he did not know.

When consciousness returned to him, his helper was still there, waiting for him and on his face rested the very same stern, accusative look.

All faint remnants of conceit and brashness vanished from Scimarajh's soul and shock slammed into him.

Silently, for the second time and yet like never-ever-before-done, he began to weep, but could not say why.

His helper let him weep, spoke not one word. Nature let him weep, made not one sound.

When he was through, he felt free.

He opened his luminous eyes and looked straight into them of his helper, and gave account of himself:

"I know not where I have placed my key, sir!"

And the face of his helper melted to yield a look of deep love, deeper than words can tell, like the harsh sun-skies melt away at nightfall to uncover yon softe moon.

"Your key, at this very moment, Scimarajh," said his helper in the most gentle and enigmatic of voices, "lies at the bottom, at the very bottom, of the Lake of Love."

Scimarajh looked into his helper's eyes and a new strength flowed into him and filled him to the very *corner* of his being.

"Really, sir?"

"Really and truly."

"But how did it get there?"

"When you get it, you will know."

"And how do I get it?"

"By diving in. Again."

Scimarajh straightened, and then the deepest of gratitude unfolded within his heart. Tear-filled, his eyes glittered like pearls as he said:

"Sir, what is you name?"

"I am your helper." Simple.

"Will I see you again?"

"That depends."

"Depends on what, my helper?"

"Depends on how you fare."

"You won't help me, then?" asked Scimarajh bravely.

"I stand by you every moment! And I am *waiting* for you..."

Scimarajh breathed softly for seconds. How could he broach his deepest thoughts? His most silent question. He could not find within him the audacity to ask it straight-off, so he approached it gradually, almost fearfully:

"Sir," he asked, "Why do you call this lake the Lake of Love?"

His helper smiled; that special, soul-strengthening smile.

"You want to know?"

"Aye!" replied Scimarajh.

"Walk to its edge and gaze into it."

Scimarajh obeyed.

"Now tell me," sounded the voice of his helper behind him. "*What* do you see?"

Scimarajh peered silently into the silver-coated lake for a long time. Finally he spoke, thoughtful:

"I see only myself, helper."

"*Only?*" asked the helper in surprise.

Scimarajh turned back to the face in his tears.

"Yes, sir," he said. "Only myself."

His helper's voice softened, became richer, echoed within the halls of Scimarajh's soul like a thousand voices:

"Is that not already a lot to see, my son?"

Scimarajh fell silent, he had no reply. Finally, after a long time, he said:

"I sense a deep mysterious truth in your statement, sir, but I must confess that I am yet to grasp it! – Surely I must see *beyond* myself to know more. I understand not."

"Your honesty shall take you there soon."

"Thank you, sir." Scimarajh hesitated. "Helper..."

"Son?"

"But if, then, this is a Lake of Love, how come I almost drowned in it? How come strange, unfriendly currents occupy its invisible depths?"

"Because *you* have made it so!"

Again an incomprehensible statement. Scimarajh looked down at his hands, at himself.

"Me??! But *how*, sir? I only just got here! I swear. I've never seen that lake before or touched it. This is odd. I do *not* understand!"

"And understand shall you still not until you have gone in again and come out. Then shall you know everything!"

Scimarajh saw the opening he had been looking for. Hesitant, yet desperate, he took it:

"So it *is* possible to get to the bottom, and resurface alive?" He inquired haltingly, tenderly.

"If it were not, my son," his helper asked in return, equally tender of voice," Would I tell you to do it?"

Scimarajh was silent for a long time. He opened his soul completely. There was no time for bravado or half-measures. The strange force in that lake was all too fresh in his memory.

His answer had to be genuine. After all was said and done, did he truly *trust* his helper?

A smile grew upon his face from the depths of his heart. And in his most true spirit he knew that never, not once ever, in his life had he known so much love and trust for anybody as he suddenly knew towards this stranger who seemed more familiar to him almost even than his own self.

Sans thoughts and spontaneously, his answer broke forth and vibrated lightly his pool of tears.

"No, sir! If it were impossible, you wouldn't bid me do it. And so the fact that *you* have told *me* to do it is the very proof of my success. I thank you, sir, for your immense love. You truly are my helper!"

As he spoke, the helper's face began to quiver and then thin away. Alarm sprang into Scimarajh's eyes. He had not noticed that his tears had been suddenly draining away into the soft, grassy soil.

"Helper!" he cried. "You're disappearing!"

His helper laughed lightly, amused.

"No, Scimarajh, I'm not."

"Yes, you are ... oh ...! Oh! No ..." The helper's face had vanished completely, his pool of tears fully drained.

"Oh, where are you?" called Scimarajh.

"I am here where I've always been," the helper's voice sounded in the air, fainter.

"But you've vanished!"

"No, I have not. The *image of my face* has vanished from *your* sight."

"Is this magic?"

"There is really *nothing* like magic, *my son...*" his voice was fading quickly.

"Oh helper, now I am alone again. I am weak. What shall I do to succeed?"

"Do *that* which you do best, Scimarajh!"

"What, helper?! What?" called Scimarajh.

"Listen to your inner voice, son..." his helper's voice seemed to be coming from miles away, borne aloft the wings of restless air-spirits, and barely audible, *"... and you shall realise what."*

"And...," Scimarajh heard him faintly continue, *"When in trouble, cry for Help, my son... - and remember,..."* each word was less audible than the last, *"this is ... the Kingdom ... of ... Honesty ...so ... always ... be*

...."

His voice had faded away completely.

Scimarajh stood on his feet for a long time, straining ears, eyes and yearning heart. Strange. He had never made such a good friend so fast, nor lost one so early. Never before in his life had he gained so much comfort, knowledge and strength from such a short conversation.

"Oh when shall I see you again?" he whispered to himself under his breath. And in his memory he heard the sonorous voice of his helper once more: *that depends ... depends on how you fare*.

Scimarajh collected himself and approached the Lake of love. He *had* to go in. But oh-so-well could he remember what it was like in there. Oh dear, what to do?

Then the words of his helper sounded in his ear. Do that which you do best.

What did he do best? Scimarajh could not figure it out. But he should! What was it that his helper believed that he did best and which would simultaneously ensure him success. He lifted his eyes to the skies thoughtfully, turning round at the same time. And *there* it was...the Land of Bliss and, over it, the rainbow and, above the rainbow, the new bird ... - it dazzled his eyes and moved his soul to worship. Pure worship. *Worship? ... that was it!* He was to pray!!

That was what he did best! Pray! How could he have forgotten?! *Oh wanderer … where is thine wisdom?*

If you think simply, you'll see the point.

Scimarajh lifted his face and hands up to heaven and prayed the most fervent prayer for help that he had ever prayed. It rushed through his entire being, nerve and bone and open soul, and surged heavenwards like a rocket of fireworks.

Amen.

He opened his eyes. Nature fell silent, and calm descended upon, if into, his soul. Calm, and the strongest resolve ever felt by him, seized him. He was not himself any longer.

Free of apprehension, consumed of power and unflinching courage, and propelled by superhuman force, he took three firm, brisk steps to the very edge of the Lake of Love.

A moment of absolute stillness. Muscles tensed.

And in he went.

Unafraid. Wanderer. Sojourner. Conqueror!

ii.

The Littlers

...

Che Chidi Chukwumerije

. . .

As soon as he penetrated the transparent torquise lake, he heard the little whispering voices inside his ears. Instinctively he knew that they were there to help him and, spontaneously, he surrendered himself to their instructions.

Good dive, they said, *now keep shooting straight.*

He followed the order and kept his body rigid. In no time he was again hit by that icy chill and then the irresistible force gripped him again, making him dizzy.

Do not pause! And do not panic, whispered the voices; *allow the force to draw you down to the bottom! Relax...*

A moment of indecision ... and then he obeyed. And to his surprise the chill eased off, his head cleared and the force ceased to hurt as he felt himself being attracted, as by a receding wave, down to the bottom.

How easy it was.

But his lungs had started to ache slightly. He had better get the key quickly and return to the world without.

His fingers touched the dark, muddy soil and he

righted himself until he floated lightly on his feet at the bottom. It was surprisingly clear, as if the water itself were luminous.

Quickly Scimarajh's eyes began to scan the lake-floor, searching for ... for *what*? And for the first time he realised that he did not even know the nature of the key for which he was searching.

Startled, running short of breath, he quickly pricked up his inner ears for to hear the whispering voices.

You're searching wrongly!, it sounded in his ears.

What was he to do, then?

Spin around! He spun, and saw ... two portals. Two round openings before him, on the lake floor. The first was shinning with light and the second was dead-black dark.

He moved towards the light one.

No! ENTER into the black hole... –

Scimarajh hesitated. The *black* hole? That could not be right. He waded towards the black and looked ... opaque and dead. A silent dread gripped him. He began to ruminate and, consequently, he became confused ~~

And his lungs were aching for air. He had by now expelled almost all the air he had dived in with. No time to debate in thought! Quick, man, make thine decision!

He took another look at the black hole and then

spun around as fast as he could and waded rashly towards the bright opening of the shinning eye. *No!!*

Too late. As soon as he tried to immerse himself in the shinning portal, a star seemed to explode in his head. Though under water, yet he screamed with pain!

A gigantic force, a hundred times more powerful that the one above, sucked him from all directions. Water rushed in through his nostrils; reality began to fade. A typhoonic cyclical current arose and began to whip him round and round, faster and faster, with dynamic force!

Death stared him straight in the face, unsmiling.

Oh, no ... was this truly the end? He could not think. He was passing out. Oh Lord, please ... then he remembered the last advice of his helper.

And with his last surge of energy, he shut his bruised eyes, concentrated totally within, and from his heart of hearts, in his heart of hearts, screamed desperately:

-       H E L P !!! -

And then the lights went out.

When he came to he was lying on the soft grass a few feet away from the bank of the Lake of Love again, tired, in mortal pain and extremely hungry.

How did he get there? *Where* was he? For some

seconds his mind was empty of comprehension; and then in an agonising rush the memory came surging back.

He remembered everything – his missing back-pack, the face in the tears, the Lake of Love, down to his last, gruesome moments therein – everything.

And with this recollection came the great question: *what* was he doing here, outside, alive? He should be inside and dead. Who had rescued him? How did he survive?

The answer could not be received and he found thinking a difficulty. He tried to raise his head but the effort caused a great deal of pain. He groaned and his head lolled back into the grass. The rays of the sun burned his eyes and made him dizzy, and his body was in no state to resist and, with a deep moan, he sank back into unconsciousness.

How long he stayed in this state he did not know, but when he woke up the sun was still bright in the sky, blinding him, and he was just as weakened, like one drugged, and searingly famished, as he had been the last time he woke.

Scimarajh groaned. His whole body ached. His eyes burned. Didn't the sun ever go down in this place? Hunger and thirst ravished him through and thorough. He moaned. Oh where was his helper? Suddenly he remembered him.

"Helper," he whispered, but completely inaudibly.

"Helper..." He waited. Nothing stirred. Leaf nor grass whispered. The wind had folded his wings.

Despair descended into his spirit like dark night. Clearly, clearly, he saw the menacing spectre of the adamantine certainty of his pitiful end. *Why?*

He could not understand. Had he not resolutely and of his own accord renounced the dark and immoral ways of men in order to determinedly seek the truth and the light? In order to re-find the Land of Bliss? The beautiful, fairy-like Land of Bliss from which, legend said, men had once, aeons upon aeons ago, journeyed to find maturity and individuality so as one day to return again -...?

And this legend had awakened a powerful echo in Scimarajh's heart. He knew it was true! There was no "proof" of it, no pictures, no recollections; nobody that he knew of had ever gone to the Bliss-Land and returned to tell him how it was there ... and *yet*, inside his soul, the unformed, vague splittings of a long-silent memory stirred and stirred up a *deep, wrenching pain*.

Strange, but, for the first time in his life, Scimarajh was filled with an intractable longing. *Longing. Oh wanderer* ... he became homesick!

Homesick? But wherefore? He was a man in the world of men, or not so? Why then this Homesickness? This strange, intangible longing which, because it was so strange and so intangible, only caused him even more pain. He wanted to go home. But where was home?

Home is where the heart is. Was his heart not here, then? With his wife, his beloved wife, and his loving children, bringers of joy? Where then could his heart be? Scimarajh wondered. He pondered. He sought. And, finally, he prayed...

Until he could delude himself no longer. The wise men could not be so wise after all, nor the priests reliable custodians of truth if they could neither substantiate nor satisfy these boundless flames flickering...nay, not flickering ... but *burning* fiercely inside his Soul!

Nor could his heart, his true heart, his heart of hearts, really be with his people or with his occupation which suddenly yielded him no more joy.

No!

So one day, oh one fateful, yea, fated morn, arising with the dawn, he shed his old world with the same finality with which day sheds the dark mantle of night, and moved out with the rising sun.

Out ... out of indolence, out of faintheartedness, out of the hearth of ignorance and arms of comfort and set off boldly, boldness supreme, to seek for truth and find his heart.

If the Land of Bliss was reality, then he was a victor, for nothing, aye nothing, would stop him.

Seven treacherous deserts defeated emphatically!

Seven wild forests shed like a garment! Seven angry seas conquered and sailed ... his longing drawing him along, his desire fuelling his drive, uncheckable, unstoppable.

Yea... *unstoppable?*

The mocking question arose silently within him like a phoenix.

If he was unstoppable then how come he lay by a simple lake now, sinking away...? Truly and really, Scimarajh comprehended not.

"Lord," he prayed within him, "I lack not in desire, nor longing, nor drive, nor *trust*. Thou seest my soul and seest that I *thirst for Life!* Please, *what* is it then which bars my way?"

And, without knowing it, he for the first time prayed for *enlightenment* and *not* just for strength, strength to act according to his own ideas.

A gentle breeze wafted over to him, cooling him down, silencing his questing thoughts. His eyes closed and he was submerged once again into a deep, deep slumber.

But this time, while he slept, he dreamt.

In his dream he saw a man with shackles round his ankles trying to climb a tree. He had travelled a long distance to get to this tree on the top branch of which blossomed the biggest, brightest fruit that Scimarajh had ever beheld.

The man tried and tried, but could not succeed in

climbing because of the shackles. So he sank down to the ground, weary and dejected.

"Hey! You!" called Scimarajh to him. "You have shackles around your feet! Unshackle yourself first, man, *then* you will easily climb the tree and pluck the beautiful fruit!"

But the man did not seem to hear him. Scimarajh called louder, but the man still heard him not. Then Scimarajh realised why. The man was talking to himself, and repeating and emitting his thoughts and prayers so loud that he was not aware of *anything* else.

"Oh, foolish man," muttered Scimarajh as he slowly reawakened from his slumber. "He neither notes that he is shackled nor bothers to find out or to truly listen! Foolish man..."

His eyes opened. *And then his eyes opened –*
Of course!

That was it. This dream was a message to him! He, too, was shackled, but inwardly so.

The sun was still out, this eternal sun, and nature remained quiet, but Scimarajh was no longer aware of them. He was occupied with his new realisation.

Before his mind's eye arose once more the picture of the shackled tree-climber. Yet all he had to do was examine *his own self* and he would see the way out of his dilemma.

The seeker and humble one in Scimarajh began to

reflect...

Before he dived into the lake the first time, nature was talking to him, but he bothered not to discover what she said ... he caught glimpses of the quick movements of little human-like beings but he did not really want to know if he had seen well...and his helper's voice had told him not to dive in, but he heeded it not ... *plus* his own inner voice had warned him but he refused to hear – and what happened?

He lost his back-pack. Why? Impatience. Self-will. Stubbornness. Brashness.

Scimarajh groaned with the pain of self-realisation. But *inside* his groan lay a smile. Ah, Sunlight...

And then he reflected on his second dive...and he remembered the little whispering voices, talking to him. He recollected how the first part of the venture had gone surprisingly smoothly as he followed the whispered instructions. And then when he disobeyed ... *bang! Crash!* Lights-out.

Again his own self-will, his own rashness, had been the cause. His lack of *self*-control. He was yet to truly conquer himself and his shortcomings, master his nature, like he had once been advised to do.

Slowly Scimarajh breathed out softly and, with the exiting breath, a heavy load seemed to slowly lift itself off his tired frame. – And then the birds began to sing and he saw them, beautiful with a beauty above human words, take wing and begin to flitter through the air. Gentle winds arose, the grass stirred and tick-led the skin of his face. The rays of the sun softened and suddenly he found that he could move. Not very well, but still he could make little movements. The Pressure that had lain over him like a bear had eased.

Tears welled up in his eyes. He was not going to die afterall.

Oh Lord ... my God - - -

But what to do now? He was weak, hungry, hurt. There was no way he could help himself, save some-body else helped him.

And yet it needed not be so! If only he had been less brash, less impetuous, less self-willed, this would never have happened. And Scimarajh vowed never again to yield to these weaknesses but to con-quer them instead. And this vow was a prayer. And the prayer was a channel through which fresh peace entered his soul. And the peace strengthened him. His thoughts became crystal-clear.

He needed his helper. He called him, still in a whis-per but this time audibly:

"Oh helper ... helper mine...please come to my res-cue." He waited a long time. Nothing happened. So he called again and waited an even longer time. Still nothing happened and, for the third time, he called. But no response. No helper. No friend.

Anew was Scimarajh baffled. His brows collected, then they brightened again. Maybe another pool of tears was needed! But as soon as this thought hit him he knew it was not right. The last time, the tears had been spontaneous and genuine; this time he would surely have to falsely stimulate or, worse, simulate them. And he was certain that a grave punishment would be meted out upon him were he to attempt any such thing. Besides that anyway, this time he was lying down facing the sky and he could not shed tears *upwards*, now *could* he?! - ? –

Scimarajh banished these thoughts from his mind. The words of his helper sounded in his ears:...*depends on how you fare.*

Obviously he was not worthy to meet his luminous helper yet. He sighed. An alternative course of action had definitely to be taken.

What?

A thought came:

The little whispering voices which had sounded in his head whilst he was yet in the lake. To whom could they perhaps belong? ... then another thought:

Could they perhaps belong to the *little things* he was almost sure he had seen from the corners of his eyes as he approached the Lake of Love the first time. For a moment he had thought he'd seen little miniature people...

Scimarajh paused in thought. Little human-like beings? What exactly was he talking about? Could there be any such thing?

He wrestled his doubt briskly to the ground.

And why not? A face in a pool of tears ... portals at the bottom of a lake ... voices in ears ... a sun that never went down ... so why could there not be any such thing as little human-like beings if there were any such things as little human-like beings? Man is often the single stranger in his own home, destructive and ignorant.

And with his doubt gone, Scimarajh was suddenly sure that the voices that had guided him in the lake belonged to the little beings, flashes of whose quick movements he had seen from the corners of his eyes as he first approached the lake. Mayhaps *they* would help him, he thought hopefully.

Then his heart softened. Even if they did not help him, at least he owed them his thanks. They had saved his life, or only attempted to. The one was as deserving of gratitude as the other.

And even before he could find it in himself to ask for their help, his gratitude found word:

"Oh I thank you all, you so tiny human-like beings; for intuitively I know that you they were who spoke to me in the water. *Thank* – "

And even before he could finish, they appeared! Tumbling out from all sides, all holes, all corners, in a symphony of mind-blowing sound-and-colour ... they appeared.

The eyes of Scimarajh bulged and almost popped

out of their sockets. What was he seeing?

Littlers, that's what he was seeing. Little, handsome ones, beautiful when the word is rightly defined, and colourfully dressed.

Smiles adorned their faces, one and all, and a certain joyous bubble permeated the atmosphere. Instantaneously Scimarajh felt filled with incredible strength and indefinable happiness.

The noise quietened. They stood looking at him expectantly with shinning eyes, an unbelievable sight. Like little reflections of human beings; little "men" and "women", princes and princesses, dashing youths and dancing maidens almost, yet more. This world is rich, but man is so blind.

"Who ... *who are you?*" sputtered Scimarajh with a stammering tongue.

Their smiles broadened, a few of them giggled and laughed. Then one stepped forward slightly until he was almost on Scimarajh's face.

"We," he said in a strangely soothing voice, "are the *little nature-workers. Not* human-like beings as such, as you've dubbed us."

"The *who*?" asked Scimarajh in childlike dazzle.

"The little *nature*-beings," the little being said. "We tried to tell you not to dive so into the Lake of Love the first time but you understood us not and attributed our voices to the rustling of restless leaves. And even though you caught glimpses of us, still you cared not to investigate!

"And we it was who tried to guide you safely to the bottoms of the lake. We instructed you to enter the black hole through which *your bag* had fallen, to retrieve it, but you went against our instructions in brash self-will! And now you're lost. And yet if you had listened and obeyed the *first* time, you would have been safely and correctly guided through your destiny…"

At first Scimarajh did not *hear* what he had just been told, but gazed in wonder at the little speaker. Even though he had already been convinced of their existence and had thanked them, still now that he was actually *seeing* them…

And yet they all looked so normal, really. –

Then the words of the little speaker suddenly registered and Scimarajh shook and was remorseful. He lowered his eyes in shame.

"I'm sorry, little nature-workers," he said in a genuinely sorry voice.

"Sorry for yourself, Scimarajh, be sorry for yourself. For you and you alone have been hurt by your actions!"

Scimarajh looked up in surprise. The words were true, but so *severe* … and then he saw that the littler was actually smiling, not frowning, even though it strangely seemed to be the reverse. And how come everybody seemed to know his name around here?

Involuntarily he too smiled and a dashing light-heartedness surged through him. He became light and talkative. He forgot that he was still lying by the side of the lake, hungry and weak. It really was as if the beings fed him with energy which he spontaneously converted –

"So how come you didn't appear this way to me all the while?" he asked.

"You didn't call us." It was another littler that answered. "You did not even believe in us."

"But how could I have believed in something I did not know about?"

The littlers shrugged.

"Who's fault that you knew of us not? Not ours. *We* know about you and your race, the humans. After all we all live in the same world." –

Scimarajh thought deeply awhile. Then he observed:

"But I did not call you just now before you came, did I?"

"Yes you did!"

"I did?" He thought back. "No, I only thanked you, that's all."

A being laughed: *"Only?"*

Another giggled: *"All?"*

"Your genuine gratitude," said the first little speaker, who by his appearance and aura seemed to be their leader, "was the most potent call you could have made. And here in the Kingdom of Honesty, what you call for with your heart, right or wrong, you get immediately."

Scimarajh fell silent. So many new pieces of wisdom received today. Gratitude assailed him anew. *He had so much to be grateful for.*

He came out of his absorption and looked at the little beings. Fatigue made itself felt again.

"I'm tired…" he softly said.

"Don't worry, Scimarajh, we'll take care of you. And we'll help you. You still have time."

"Time? For what?"

"To prepare for your last journey into the Lake of Love," replied the little nature-worker. "But for now you need care and that's why we're here, to help you if you'll let us, sir."

Scimarajh stared at the little human-like being – or *nature-being*, rather. He had so many questions. Who were they? Why did they describe themselves as nature-workers? What did they mean by he still "having time"? Why exactly was this lake called the Lake of Love? How did *his* key get to the bottom of the lake, the heart of love and, hence, its unravelling, if he, intuiting, was right? Where was his helper? How come the sun never went down? …questions, questions and more questions.

Obviously they would have to wait, for the little nature-workers had gone into action. Laughing and sprity, they surrounded him closely, pressing against every part of him. Then suddenly, as though he were weightless, he felt himself being lifted into the air.

"Am I not too heavy?" he asked weakly.

They laughed.

"Unity overcometh all obstacles. Always remember that, Human!"

They began to move, taking him...*where?* He knew not, nor minded. He just relaxed, knowing that he was in safe hands.

His head began to swim and, gratefully, he fell asleep.

He awoke on a comfortable divan of soft hay, framed in hard, gleaming wood. Over and around him stood strong, sturdy trees, providing shade and cool, and beautiful fragrances delighted his senses. He must be in the woods, he realised.

He felt much stronger and sat up gently. He was hungry. And alone.

No, not alone. There beside him was a beautiful spread of delicious, ripe fruits. A smile crossed his face and he was grateful.

Slowly he began to satiate his hunger, wondering where his little friends were.

He had almost finished when some of them came trotting out from behind him, three they were, each holding a cup of water.

"Hello, Scimarajh. Did you enjoy your meal?"

He assured them truthfully that he had never tasted more delicious or refreshing fruits in his whole life.

They handed him the water and he drank thirstily. It was cool and instantly invigorating. He had never *tasted* water so good before.

"Is this water?" he asked when he was done. The three little cups had been exactly enough.

"Men have polluted the waters in their vicinity," answered one of the little beings, "the water graciously made available to them by the Supreme Ruler! You no longer know what values, how great, pure water has, and is."

Scimarajh agreed without any doubt. He looked about him curiously.

"I have so many questions," he said quietly.

"Yes," they said, "Men always do."

"Is it wrong, then, to ask questions?" Scimarajh demanded in surprise. "Surely to learn new things questions must be asked, and answered."

"If men were humbler, simpler and more straightforward in their thinking and actions they would have very few questions because already they would have observed *much, much, much* that today escape their shallow attention!"

Scimarajh reflected. New questions arose but he uttered them not. Maybe he should try to find the answers out by himself first.

"Good," they said.

The seeker looked up. "Pardon?"

"We said that that is a good intention."

"What intention?"

"To attempt to find the answers *personally*."

Scimarajh looked at them, shocked.

"How do you know what I'm *thinking*? I said nothing!"

"What are words when we can see your thoughts?" they chanted in a melodious sing-song.

"You can *see my thoughts*?"

"Clearly, like pictures, we see your thoughts as they arise and take on form. Your mind can be likened to the sky, and your thoughts to the stars, the clouds, the rainbows and to all the other entities that live in the sky.

"We see them when they first appear, like faraway stars; we see the bright happy thoughts like suns, and the ugly self-willed ones become grey clouds, while the evil ones are black holes, extinguishing all light and life. And the sad, confused ones are soon fluffy clouds floating by which temporarily block the blue firmament and yet do not resist the penetrating radiance of the sun: they are confused alright but if you do not cling unto but let them alone they soon float away. But when you dwell on them they become dark clouds, *heavy with rain*, weighing down your soul!"

"And like the moon are your thoughts of reflection

and contentment, the bright yellow moon. But your most beautiful thoughts are your worship-thoughts. They appear as mighty rainbows arching dynamically and uncheckably towards and into heaven.

"And once in a while, even, Scimarajh, we see an angel in your thoughts, an angel and a dove...winging their way through thine skies. God loveth thee, wanderer. Ask thyself, art thou worthy of such Love?" –

Nine eternities of silence passed by. Scimarajh wept but knew not that he did so, or why. Then, softly, the littler continued:

"Oh yes, Scimarajh, the thoughts of men are clearly visible to us. And that is why we help you so willingly. For, of all yesterday's men, you have come the farthest yet in your quest for purity."

Modesty had found its way into Scimarajh's heart! Modesty, humility and the awareness of his own unworthiness! And the joy of a new knowledge: *thoughts are visible!* Then there are no secrets in life! No secrets. He thought back into the world of men, their hypocrisies which they tag diplomacy; their lying and plotting ways, and his heart was breaking, breaking for them. Poor fellow humans.

"We leave you to your thoughts now, Scimarajh. When you need us again we shall come. For now we have other work to do."

And in a flash they had dashed off. Scimarajh gazed after their departing forms in a trance.

He spent his period of solitude in deepest reflection. If thoughts are visible then truly men can never deceive God. That realisation amused him so much that he finally began to laugh.

He quietened and new arenas of knowledge began to open up within him. But, mostly, the *old* questions still cried for answers.

Shortly he fell asleep again. He awoke. He became slightly restless. Cautiously he got up unto his feet on the soft forest grass.

For a while he felt dizzy, then his head cleared. He began to take gentle strides through the beautiful clearing where his little helpers had taken him.

Content he was.

Then he heard footsteps behind him. Turnèd he and saw the leader of the little nature-workers there behind him standing.

"Oh hullo!" he called in spontaneous joy.

His childlike joy aroused friendly happiness in the little being.

"Scimarajh!" he called back.

Scimarajh walked up to him and sat down on the grass. The nature-worker sat down beside him. For some time they both said nothing. They seemed to be old, time-weathered friends, as comfortable in silence as they were in speech.

Finally the little worker spoke:

"So, tell me, Scimarajh: what brings you here?"

"But you know that already. You can see my Thoughts."

The worker laughed. And he laughed.

"You *are* a receptive human being!" declared he.

"I have heard enough today to humble me truly and I have reflected upon them. But I must confess that I still have lots of questions."

"Unburden your mind, human!" said the nature-one.

"Thank you, sir. My first questions concern you and your folk. *How* be ye little *nature workers*, and wherefore?"

His eyes were serious, a spirit in quest.

And the little elemental being began to explain in a grave voice:

"There is only *One* God. He owns everything that is. His Spirit Which is Holy created all the world and put two different types of beings therein: the guests, like you, who only need to venture through the worlds experiencing and learning, but also ennobling. And the workers, like us, who tend, form and nurture nature and the structures of the creations.

"We both are servants, but of different kinds. The wind, the seas, the shifting mountains, nature, fire and all other elemental substance are in our care. We execute the Will of the Supreme Ruler in the world and are happy to do so. For we are *elemental beings!*

"You human spirits, you human beings, however,

have the duty to study our activity and, in enjoying it, not to hinder, but to further it. *Thus* will you know joy. You are guests; we are workers. And yet *all of us are all* workers, for every creature is a servant! *We* be of different sizes. Some of us are *so* big that, for the size, you could hardly see them –

"Giants who care for celestial bodies and suns, for whole oceans and vast mountain-ranges. But some are small. Amongst these are the tiny master-weavers who work with the emitted thoughts of men, planting and watering them like seeds so that each man will reap without fail the multiple fruits of the seeds he secretly sows. Or we take care of natural forms – another group of us Littlers – flowers, stones, small animals, lakes ... we care for them lovingly. And there *are* so many many others and types.

"But human beings have become blind. They see us no longer, nor know about us, yet they were friends with us long ago. But no more. They still know our names, yes, fairies, fays, gnomes, elves, littlers, nixies, sprites, salamanders, mermaids, dryads, and so on and ever on, but now they have relegated us to the unreal sphere of fables and legends. They doubt our existence, you men of today – because men have become darkened with evil and blinded by impurity, over millennia. Yet we still are *here*! And because men have separated themselves from us, they can no longer receive gifts or instructions or warnings from us. And only they will suffer for that. Never us.

"For we are free and unsoiled. We serve the Light, and Him Alone, and paradise forever resides with us, the nature-workers, the invisible animistic servants in life!"

Scimarajh listened like one spellbound; or rather: one freed from a spell. Transfixed and untransfixed. *Wow...!*

And he had never *known* of them before! For a long time he raised his eyes in wonderment and bright thought. When he lowered them eyes, the littler was long gone.

Scimarajh did not mind. He had heard enough with which to occupy himself for the next time-span. Now so many things made sense: the *origins* of fairy-*tales*; the regulating, obvious yet unsurmised, force within nature; the superstitions of men, foolish or real; and lots more. Where there is smoke there is fire. Sometimes. *But there is always a source!*

In this way a long time passed again. He began to feel fresh hunger pangs and instinctively he walked back to the lovely divan. And *what* did he see!

Beautiful, ethereal *female* nature-beings. Feminine workers. Passive handlers. They *floated*...and from the backs of their shoulders quivered light-permeated wings; *beautiful*.

Involuntarily a cry of delight escaped Scimarajh's lips. Beauty truly is an elixir of spirit!

They looked up at him with observant eyes and smiled gently at him, asking him to come and partake of the meal which they had prepared for him. For a moment he did not move, paralysed by their tender severity.

Then he noticed the food and obeyed. He sat down on the divan and gazed at it. He had never seen anything like it before but it called to him.

The little maidens left and he began to eat, reflecting on the rarefied female littlers. Their nature and being defied words. It was as though they caught the rays of the sun within them and then reflected their radiance out again, modified, intensified. Everything about them breathed Truth and *Purity*. –

But the taste of the food soon claimed his contemplation as well. Scimarajh could honestly say that he had never tasted anything better. Eaten anything more strengthening. Again it struck him how anything prepared by the nature-workers differed so refreshingly from all the works of men.

When he was through he drank the water which they had left behind in large quantities. Then sleep overcame him.

A happy noise woke him up after the refreshing snooze.

He saw beings playing and laughing. They invited him to join in their games and he did so. Happily did they play.

After the games they took him on a tour of the woods. They showed him the clear, rippling spring from where they fetched him the cool, invigorating water he loved to drink and in the travelling water he saw his waving reflection watching him, and he remembered the Lake of Love. They showed him a distant circle of rare animals and he closed his eyes in joy, and his joy was a prayer-of-gratitude to Him, God the Father, the Supreme, aye, the One. –

They showed him beautiful flower-cups in which little miracles slept, waiting to one day soon grow and overtake the world. They showed him the hidden tunnels through which garden- and soil gnomes voyaged to get to their secret domains beneath the surface of the Kingdom, where they carried out secret duties.

They showed him, yes the showed him so *many* things, the most indescribable, not with these words of mine. Highs and lows and points of change. Fairies painting in the eternal sky, and salamanders dancing in awakening fire and stretching the flickering flames, now high, now low. They even showed him how our world shifts...-

And finally they permitted and invited him to join in some of their work. He did. All he had to do was follow their instructions, and it was as easy as child's play –

And when they had wandered for a long time,

laughing and chatting and working, Scimarajh observed that they had again returned to his own "house".

The leader of this little band of elemental beings was standing lithely on the divan, awaiting him. He was wearing a green cap which, Scimarajh would finally know, symbolised wisdom.

As the other little beings dispersed, their ancient leader smiled and said:

"They are very happy and excited to see you and play with you, Scimarajh. It has been a very long time since a human being last came this way."

Then he set off with Scimarajh on a gentle stroll, his green cap upon his head. Seriousness descended upon them. A deep graveness. After all the fun and laughter, Scimarajh sensed that a period of intense education was about to follow.

And he was happy. He had many questions. *Real* questions.

The traveller wondered if he could speak first. The littler had said nothing still; he only sang a soft melody under his breath, to himself. With difficulty the human being curbed his impatience. Finally the green-capped leader turned.

"Scimarajh?" said the elemental being.

"Yes?"

"What do you intend to do when you finally get into the Land of Bliss?" Question.

Scimarajh thought.

"I need a rest," said he, and then stopped short. "Or *do I*?" he queried himself.

"Answer yourself."

"I do not know," continued Scimarajh. "But I'll request to see the King and I'll tell him my story." Answer.

The green-capped littler's voice changed, sounded strange:

"Then you surely are not yet ready!" Judgement.

"I'm not? Why?" The Search.

Search, brother, *search!*

"When you know why, then you'll be ready. *I could never tell you.* But now *Time* is ready," the being glanced up into the sky.

"Time?" Scimarajh followed his eyes. "But the sun never goes down here."

"Time has nothing to do with the sun," said the elemental one; "Time stands still, and the sun is just another traveller, but constant in its nature and travels, unlike man..." He paused a while and then added: "And yes, the sun *does* go down here."

"When?" asked Scimarajh in surprise, after assimilating the curious thing that the Littler had just said about Time.

"Each time you sleep," replied the being, "then for you a sun goes down."

"Really?"

"And truly."

Scimarajh reflected.

"But I'm not feeling sleepy now. So how come my time is ready?"

The little being pointed:

"Look! The other sun is about to begin its descent. Night calls it. Soon you must dive again into the Lake of Love."

And suddenly Scimarajh realised that they had arrived at the end, or start, of the woods, and there in front of them lay the calm lake.

The Lake of Love.

Something jumped in Scimarajh soul. What it was, he did not know.

The Lake of Love. Captor of his back-pack and of his key to the Shinning Silver Gate of the Singing Land of Solemn Bliss...

"Do you know what bliss means?" It was the little worker speaking.

"It means complete rest," answered Scimarajh promptly.

"Are you sure?"

"Could it mean anything else, anything less?" queried the wanderer.

"Wanderer, wanderer," said the elemental, "have you been so actively astir all these years only in order to slump into new inactivity? Did you laboriously free yourself from indolence and inactive comfort only so as to sink back into it? *Think!"*

Scimarajh thought. Then asked:

"What *is* bliss, then, sir?"

"When you know you shall know, but for now cure yourself of the delusion that bliss is inactivity!"

Scimarajh was quiet. Then asked urgently, for suddenly he was seized with a powerful urgency:

"Why, littler, exactly is this lake called the Lake of Love?"

"Look into it!"

Again! Scimarajh truly was baffled. His reflection again.

"I see myself."

"You *do?*"

"Yes I do."

"Then how come you ask the silly question?"

"Please, wise one, I comprehend not!"

"And shall not, until you have gone in and again returned."

Again! The same reply again. Why?

Scimarajh became more urgent. Increasingly it was dawning on him that the time he had spent with the littlers had been but a respite to help him recover his strength and also learn lessons. Suddenly the time seemed *so short!*

Lessons! What lessons had he learnt?! – to be patient and not to be self-willed. To follow the proddings of his inner voice and to trust the little beings of nature, beauty and truth. Yes? What else? Was that enough? What of the key? His helper? The lake?

He needed knowledge that would help him sail through.

"Nature-worker?" called he.

"Yes?"

"Scimarajh is afraid."

"Afraid? Why?"

"The lake is mysterious. How do I get to the bottom? What is this key? And my helper – he told me he'd be with me every moment, yet he has gone. Can I truly go in and come out alive?"

The little being looked at him earnestly.

"The lake is not mysterious. *You* are mysterious, very mysterious, Scimarajh, and that is why the simplicity of the Lake of Love escapes your unnecessarily complicated mind.

"You will get to the bottom safely and return successfully, mission accomplished, if you *listen and obey* without your customary noisy thought-interference. We *are* with you, for you are earnest and good.

"The key is the key and you shall recognise it when you have possessed it, for it is *your own key* and *you* know it, except that you have *forgotten*. But if you heed our guidance you shall finally remember, when *all* is complete and round.

"And as for your helper...- Scimarajh, your helping

guide is patiently, patiently waiting for you to come to him, for he is not separated from you but you from him!"

What does a man do with knowledge when his ignorance still enshrouds thick his senses? What is truth? What is simplicity?

Scimarajh quietened his thoughts. Obviously the answer would only be attained through whatever struggle he was going to, indeed *had to*, experience at the bottom of this strange lake.

Love. *What* is love?

The little elemental being saw Scimarajh's thoughts, and Scimarajh knew.

They beheld one another. Verily, the sun had started walking towards the horizon, Scimarajh perceived.

Calm became he. Calm, so calm. And, truly, calm became him: Spirit.

They said a thousand things to one another with just that one look, the tall human and the little elemental. A thousand things. Friendship is the sea that flows twixt two islands, washing substance from one soil to the other. *Oh wanderer .... wherefore art thou?*

Scimarajh turned round and gazed pin-point sharp at the Land of Bliss. One last time. He saw the golden walls encircling the high, luminous domes ... he saw the Shinning Silver Gate, shut, shut fast, and yet inviting...he saw the giant rainbow curving dynamically over the Land ... and he saw the peculiar new bird and, again, his eyes closed and his spirit ascended in prayer, humble prayer.

And, for a fresh time, the power descended into him, a flaming, unending Arrow. Perhaps a sparrow. The Call of tomorrow. – Scimarajh opened his eyes, depthless eyes, and turned around.

All that remained were just the Lake of Love and his Soul. He started towards it and stood at its edge.

Scimarajh. Sojourner. Truth-seeker. Fighter.

He was about to go into the lake for the *last* time, *he knew,* and this time he was either going to get to the bottom or he was going to die. No half-way line again. *Either...or* -! That was all. For at the bottom of the Lake of Love lay his Key to the Shinning Gate; and if he did not get it, then he was dead anyway. Dead on the inside. Another Mortal. *Lord, be with me...*

The little elemental being stood there, long, silent, tears in his eyes, and a smile, and gazed at the spot in the water through which Scimarajh had just dived, determined.

The lake was silent. A little ripple sought the edges.

Scimarajh had disappeared into the Lake of Love.
For the last time.
Lord, be Thou with me!

iii.

The Lake of Love

...

Che Chidi Chukwumerije

...

STRENGTH SURROUNDED Scimarajh as soon as his body surged beneath the surface of the water. He perceived this strength and opened himself to it.

It filled him like liquid fire.

He was calm and clear-minded. Also clear-sighted. 'Tis funny: No matter how much trepidation has assailed the warrior before the battle, *once* he comes face to face with death, *the warrior is - - -*

Scimarajh knew that this *last* journey was decisive. It was here and now that his last questions would be answered. He had lessons to learn, apart from retrieving his bag and key. Or were the lessons directly connected with that *one* act?

He was not completely certain.

But he was determined not to let *anything* pass him by. So he opened his eyes.

Because he had done it before, succeeding through the first part was no problem. The icy cold surrounded him again and he was dizzy.

He intuitively recognised *this* familiar sensation and confidently relaxed as the strong, friendly force gripped him roughly, yet gently, and drew him along towards his destiny. And, immediately, the force and cold and dizziness disappeared and he sank trouble-lessly down to the muddy soil at the bottom.

The voices were constantly in his head and he act-ed quickly but without haste, obeying instantaneous-ly. His body was strong, exceedingly strengthened by his stay with the nature-workers; and also he had drawn a deep breath before plunging in.

He saw the two portals again and without hesita-tion heeded the voices he had once disobeyed and waded towards the black hole. He looked into it.

Pitch-black. Nothing.

Scimarajh, inspite of himself, still shuddered. He hesitated. He had to go in. He knew that no matter how scary and dark it was, he *had* to go in! For those were his orders –

Move! Now! Stop thinking! – the voices sounded in his ears. And he yielded. Immediately.

He submerged himself into the black hole at the bottom of the Lake of Love.

Scimarajh conquered his fear.

It was as though he had entered a tunnel. No, it was not just *as though*, but he *had* entered a tunnel. *Pitch*-black.

He held his heart strong and pressed inwards. Surprisingly he was not even a little out of breath. It was as if by following the instructions whispered by the little voices he entered into an unnoticed rhythm that regulated both the progress of his journey and the rate of consumption of energy within him so that he did not run so quick out of breath.

He wondered how long the tunnel stretched; while simultaneously, from the direction in which he was coming, a strong pressure told him quite clearly that he could not go back. Not that he wanted to.

But this endless, dark tunnel … ? Fear attempted to seize him anew, but he boldly shunned it. He shrugged as he slowly sank deeper, the pressure in his ear-drums building up.

If his little friends and his inner voice had told him to go into it, then it was neither endless nor would it lead him into Dark, no matter how dark the path.

With this thought any lingering threads of fear disconnected from him and a light, a small light, appeared far down at the end of the tunnel.

He progressed steadily towards it and, as he neared it, his lungs began to ache.

Relax. Panic not; sounded the voices gently in his heart.

Finally the dark tunnel widened, brightened and then Scimarajh came to the region of light, the end of the dark tunnel.

He began to feel a gentle warmth surround him as he entered into the soft, golden light at the end of the tunnel. Even strength filled him anew, although he was acutely aware of the fact that he was running short of breath. Too, his ear-drums , they pounded.

He found himself in ... *a cave*!

A beautiful cave. *Beautiful.* "Cave" was not the right word for the place to which the tunnel led – "palatial chamber" was more like it.

Scimarajh's eyes bulged. He saw...

Gold, silver, emeralds, diamonds, jewels, beautiful ornaments, decorating the place. Enough to enrich the world without! And nestling here unknown at the bottom of the Lake of Love.

His own precious stones paled in beauty when compared to these –

And as soon as he thought this very thought, he saw his weathered leather bag...

The key to the Shinning Gate was forgotten!!

Scimarajh went to his bag, it was open. He saw his three *precious* precious stones, fruits of his dogged perseverance and his love, and he saw his garments.

And then Scimarajh saw, all of a sudden, another bag beside his own. More beautiful, bigger, worthier to be presented with pride, and in it were *six* of the most beautiful jewels of this cave, and a robe of the most extraordinary beauty.

Scimarajh immediately reached for the glittering bag, forgetting his own faithful, simple one.

And within him an inner voice warned! – an almost inaudible inner voice.

But he heard it. And stopped. A long Stop! One Moment of Indecision. One Moment in Time … - the old confusion seized him anew and began to make things dizzy again…

Man! Make your decision! Fast!

One last chance…

And he decided. ~

Simple.

Boldly and with a sudden certainty, Scimarajh tore his eyes away from the glittering bag and reached for his own humble pack, voice of his true spirit!

Everything began to happen in what seemed to be slow motion. He slowly extended his hand, his fingers reaching for his own humble back-pack.

Suddenly everything came to him in clear pictures which awakened within him the right concepts of everything.

He saw his journey, how and where he obtained the three gems, the bag, the garments. Each episode had been an event that jolted his pride in some way or the other and humbled him. Humility. And here again he had almost discarded it and reached for the glittery bag of the world which satisfied his greed, his lusting personal acquisitiveness, and his vanity also.

What then was the point in everything? Why had he learned those lessons about life through those three rough sections of his life?

Scimarajh eyes could see straight into his open bag, yet his fingers could not reach it. It was as though an invisible barrier stood in between. Why?

This is the heart of Love-Lake!

He was forced to keep on reflecting! Keep on seeking! *Here* lay the key to the mystery.

First he saw the garment. How had he acquired it? When he renounced the world of men and was setting off on his journey, the most beautiful clothes he had possessed had been taken along with him, to hide his bodily ugliness and so as to arrive the Bliss-Country as a prince, well-clad and well-respected.

But that desire had been only the product of conceit. The Land of Bliss is not just a place but also a *consistency*. That is to say, to get into it one not only must get there but must also *become* like they are who live there.

And they are humble. They are simple. They are not conceited and not presumptuous. Each one comes before his Lord the way he is and unveils his true soul. Even if this soul were to be ugly – which it never *could* be, *in* Heaven, however – he would not try to conceal this ugly core under a falsely impressioning garment of beauty: the true seeker must, thus, confess his sins by showing himself as he is. He does not try to be a hypocrite. He tries to outstrip his faults, yes, but those ones he still has he does not pretend not to have but *Confesses* them so that they may become open to eyes and words and experiences that could help him be rid of them finally.

But Scimarajh did not know this. He was a seeker, sure, but ignorant, and carried along with him all them caged vanities of the world. And his ego had to be therefore constantly bruised and this vanity shown clearly to him. And that had been the reason for all he had gone through.

First: the seven deserts. In crossing the deserts one by one, all his food and drink had been exhausted. His poor horse died. His clothes had become torn and tattered. This had caused him unbearable anguish because of his plans for his possessions.

And by the time he had traversed the last desert, by which time years had passed, *all* his possessions were gone.

How ironic. He had to watch them slowly rot and die away. And all he had were but the tattered clothes he was wearing. And he met the first beggar he had seen since he began his questing wanderings. And the beggar was naked.

And Scimarajh did the first selfless deed which he ever had done in his whole life. He tore off a part of his cloak and gave it to the beggar.

And the beggar turned into a prince who gave to Scimarajh two beautiful gems – one for having learnt to be simple and the second for having become selfless.

And Scimarajh travelled on until he came to the forests. Seven forests.

It was here that he encountered demons for the first time in his life and almost fled. Each demon and every wild beast was wilder than the one before it.

Scimarajh had wanted to flee but there was nowhere to flee to – there is never anywhere to hide – because he was lost in the heart of the forests. Until the demons and beasts that tormented him had seen the jewels in the clothes.

Their eyes gleamed. They reached for the gems. And in Scimarajh something snapped for the first time. Or was it that something awakened?

He resisted and fought the demons.

And – what do you know? – as his indignation and courage rose, and as he attacked the demons they melted away and fled. And thus did he keep on boldly combating each freshly hideous beast he saw until he had moved through all seven forests. And the battles strengthened him tremendously such that by the time he had also traversed the forests he had gained in fearlessness and strength.

And at the last gate leading out of the seventh forest, he saw that it was being guarded by a monster on whose forehead glowed a precious stone.

And the monster told him that the stone was the third precious stone awaiting whoever was headed for the Land of Bliss. But that to get there the person had to first go through this seventh forest gate. But only such a one could go through it who could and did defeat him in battle. Then the gem was also his.

So Scimarajh did battle with the monster. He applied all the skill he had gathered in his previous battles. *He did not once show fear.* He was strong. And finally the monster lay dead at his feet. And Scimarajh extracted the gem from his forehead, the fruit of his fearlessness; his strength; his determination; and he exited the seventh forest.

Then he came to the seas. Seven seas. Roaring like an orchestra of angry thunders.

How was he supposed to cross them?

And then he saw a mighty mansion. It was the house of the master of the sea. And he had ships for sale. That is, for sail. Did the returning wanderer want to buy?

Yes.

But ... *oh* ... how was he to pay? With his jewels?

Seemed so, said the master of the sea.

But Scimarajh could not part with these precious stones now, each of which symbolised something definite to him. - simplicity, selflessness and courage.

No.

The only alternative left, he learnt, was if he worked for the master of the sea who needed domestic help then. That way he would finally earn the worthe with which to pay for a ship.

So Scimarajh became a servant! He who had never served anybody before...

And he saw that it is not easy to serve. To serve meaneth humble to be and to work with full gratitude in one's heart for the job which one needs. Needs not just because of the payment but moreso because *only work gives a human being self-respect, a sense of fulfilment, and value,* in creation. To serve means to be discerning, to learn to understand the nature of one's master, what he needs, what he dislikes, and to adjust one's self accordingly. To serve is to conquer yourself.

And the master demanded hard work! He was unrelenting and severe. And yet, beneath his unyielding attitude, he was also extremely kind and full of love.

He ensured that Scimarajh never lacked. That he had enough to eat and a bed on which to sleep. And finally Scimarajh, who had only started working in a mechanical bid to earn money, grew to love his work and his master.

In the evenings they sat together by the fire-side-place and the master of the sea told him stories about the worlds at the bottom of the sea – the fishes, animals, plants, homes. He told Scimarajh stories about how the sea was before men became evil, when men and fishes were friends, and men used to be led by mermaids, upon the backs of sea-animals, to the bottom to see treasures that they could take.

And he also told Scimarajh about one beautiful continent that once floated on an ocean where pure and near-perfect human beings had lived and blossomed. And about how they became slowly vain when they saw that no other race in the world could compare to them in development!

And, under their last king, they started to arrogate to themselves the titles of "gods". They fought the giant invisible helpers given by God to help them, and they disregarded their women. And it is especially wrong to look down upon woman because, through her very own peculiar nature, she exercises a stronger influence on descendants. So if woman permits herself to be suppressed and allows it to affect her, then descendants will be gradually more and more imperfect.

So the Almighty gave the king and the people time to change. But when, after many years, they had not, the moon came closer to the earth in anger, and the Almighty instructed him, the master of the sea, to unleash the waters of the sea upon this realm.

And he did obey. And it was swallowed up by the great ocean. And even today it still lay there at the bottom of the bottom of the living sea...

But people do not know or do not believe this anymore.

Scimarajh asked the master how come he could control the sea so easily, and the master said to him. "I and the sea are of the same nature. When I conquer the sea I conquer my nature, and when I conquer my nature I conquer the sea. – You, Scimarajh, must learn to master yourself, then will your gifts truly serve you well."

And Scimarajh was happy living with and working for the master of the sea such that when finally, one day, the master told him that he had now earned enough worthe with which to buy himself a ship good enough to safely across the sea, Scimarajh felt sorrow even with joy.

He had been sowing a beautiful garment with a piece of cloth he had seen in the master's house, and also weaving a leather-bag. He begged the master to permit him, Scimarajh, stay a few more days in order to finish up the garment and bag, as gift to him the master.

But the master of the sea refused. Scimarajh maturing, said he, was the latter's best gift to him. And he said also that once anybody had gotten *what* he *needed* somewhere, the law of the life stipulated that he *move on* immediately!

So Scimarajh set sail aboard the big ship. From the dock he cast one last yearning look back towards the shinning Sea-castle on the all-shores of the true-sea. The master of the sea was waving at him. A tear dropped from his eye as he waved back. Then he turned around and faced his journey.

And what a journey it was! Sea-animals ... mermaids ... monsters ... almost getting capsized ... and many other adventures! But, in the end, he had sailed through ...and they had been not one but *seven* seas in all!

And Scimarajh weighed anchor on the other shores of his vast journey and descended the ship. He stepped upon dry land with only his three jewels – simplicity, selflessness and courage.

And what did he see before him but a shinning Sea-castle, a mighty mansion, identical with the master of the sea's. And, with excitement, Scimarajh approached.

And who did he see inside *but the master himself!*

A cry of joy.

A happy reunion.

And the master sombrely handed over to Scimarajh completed the very bag and garment that Scimarajh had wanted to make for him. The master was smiling with joy. Scimarajh broke down and wept.

For these objects had been the fruits of his humility, his gratitude and his desire to serve; and now they were being returned to him as gifts ... Aye, Scimarajh wept.

And then, a moment of fare-wells, of partings, and these two friends separated again- The master of the sea climbed his ship upon his sea and returned to the other side of the great ocean while Scimarajh turned eastwards and set off for the mountain-ranges in the distance.

And in both their hearts were locked secrets of friendship, memories of dear moments, and longings of love that never ever again would depart.

Friendship *is* the sea that travels twixt two happy souls, moved hearts, pure shores, wherever they may be, here and forever hereafter – hoping and reflecting, until early this morning he stood atop the little plateau and looked across the valley at the Land of Bliss...

The beauty of life is in the movement, in the adventure, in the experiencing, in the lesson being learnt.

As all these reflections roamed lightning-fast the yearning heart of Scimarajh, wisdom descended but clean into his soul. Now he understood everything. So this was what his helper meant, and the nature-workers too.

Now he knew what his key was. It was not an object but the accumulated result of the simplicity, selflessness, courage, humility, ability to be grateful and wish to serve...qualities that he had acquired laboriously through his journeys. Now he knew what his bag and its contents really signified. *They* were his key to paradise –

Or rather, they were the symbol of his true key to paradise, which key nestled inside his soul...his spirit. His humble, when living, spirit.

And immediately the barrier, the invisible barrier that prevented his hand from touching his bag, disappeared.

His fingers touched ... he grabbed his bag. Immediately he heard music. The music. The cave came alive. He saw activity. And *the other bag, the false, glittering one* ... it turned into a snake and slithered hastily away and dead.

Scimarajh smiled.

He lifted his bag, bound it shut briskly, and then for the first time noticed a gem, a flashing jewel, that had been hidden *under* his bag. It had the *shape of a key*...and immediately he knew it was his!

Happiness filled him to the point of bursting and he reached for the little flashing jewel of a key. So *there really was* a solid key to the solid Gate. Scimarajh was glad.

The little flashing key seemed to give a little soundless cry that manifested in a prolonged and intensified richening of colour, and it leapt into his approaching fingers.

Scimarajh turned to go, mission accomplished. He had his back-pack and his key ... *and his answers, his deeper key!*

And, accordingly, he had run out of breath and his eardrums seemed like they would burst at any moment!

Above, slightly, and to the right, he saw the shinning portal again, and, one distance away, the dark one. And in his heart he knew: *the shinning eye this time...*

He started towards it, his lungs crying for air.

And then something new inside him suddenly made him turn his head to the left ... and he saw ... - ! Scimarajh saw...

A man wrestling with a hideous monster, and the monster had overpowered the man and was about to swallow him up. Scimarajh became free of thoughts!

Instantly, without thinking, he surged towards the twin figures, filled with only one urge: *help!* – and he, too, had become another helper. He moved...

And as he moved he was only dimly aware that his bag had slipped away from his grasp again.

He arrived the scene and, like an angel of light, grabbed the monster by the hair and yanked it up. *And gasped –*

It was *his* face! Hideously distorted, yes, but his, Scimarajh ... and yet *not* his. Not him! Yet him! *His face! A monster had his face.*

The monster was grinning. It seemed to know what effect it was having on Scimarajh. It lifted its hand with its sharp, ugly claws and prepared to strike Scimarajh...

- Scimarajh went into action! He did not know who this monster was or what it represented. All he knew was that, no matter how much it looked like him, *it was not him!*

And if he did not kill it, then it would kill him. A simple law. And Scimarajh struck! His left hand shot out straight at the left side of the monster's chest where his heart-box lay; and the key in Scimarajh hand pierced the dark, crooked flesh there.

The monster rigidified. His mouth opened and an ugly black and yellow liquid seeped out from it.

Instinctively, following natural patterns, Scimarajh turned the key in the monster's heart the way one turns a key in a lock, then pulled out and watched...

The monster began to quake and vibrate, and then he broke apart into pieces and *vanished*! –

A new tone suffused those waters at the bottom of this strange lake.

Scimarajh turned to the figure on the floor of the lake...and again he gasped!

It was his helper!

His helper.

What was he doing here at the bottom of the Lake of Love, being wrestled to death by a monster that bore a distorted version of his, Scimarajh, face? ... !?

Nor did he have the time to reflect about that now. His time had run out! He could not go one more moment without air...

And his helper? - !

Into Action!

Scimarajh picked up his helper. His face was swollen. His eyes had rolled up. Oh, no, not his helper. Not him. Dread and frustration, fear and anxiety, and sorrow, seized Scimarajh, our wandering spirit.

He headed towards the portals...

The dark portal had disappeared and all the hero saw was just one big, wide, shinning round door above his head. As he approached it, he caught sight of his bag on the floor, drifting towards the insides of the cave.

He followed his inner voice and ignored his bag. For his helper.

And he knew that his helper was near death. *Any second* delayed would mean disaster!

Scimarajh stood beneath the ring of light, in compliance to the heavenly little voices in his inner ears which suddenly he could hear again. For, ever since he had entered the cave, they had been full silent.

And a gigantic swirl of luminous radiance gushed through the light-ring, through the water, and he suddenly felt himself being sucked upwards into the portal with the helpless body of his helper. And...

Bang!! His flashing key was knocked out of his grasp. *Oh no! Not his key!!!*

And as soon as this feeling hit him his grasp on his helper's body loosened and he began to sink away. And the swirl of light dimmed, and the force that was sucking him up left him...

It was as though nature and life were letting him

decide what to do. Deeper and to the left he saw the flashing key almost on the floor again … and there, floating away by his right, was his helper…

Who to go for? His helper or his key? Which was more important? He listened for the little voices – nothing. Silence. Now it was between him and his God. The key had hit the bottom, flashing quietly… his helper was slipping fast away … his helper … his swollen face … his open eyes … those eyes …

No!

Scimarajh was crying as he cast one more look at the little flashing jewel of a key at the bottom of the lake. Nothing made sense to him anymore. He could not even understand himself again. A strong-willed, third-eyed stranger seemed to have arisen in, and taken over, him. He wanted his back-pack, needed his key…but he could not let his helper die, a victim of a monster that had strangely borne *his* face. Every-thing within him cried *intuitively* against this! Sorry.

Had his helper not once told him that even *he* had a helper? Was Scimarajh this helper, it flashed through him? Had his helper been subtly preparing him for *this* moment…? This last act?

And, with this realisation, power and courage seized our wanderer afresh. His past was forgot-ten. All his dreams united into this one spot. Only the present mattered to him, and the future which opened up from this present!

And for now the present was wrapped up in this human being in front of him so close to death, if not already *too* close!

That it was his helper strangely did not even matter any more. It made no difference to him. At this moment *he* was helper, and a true helper sacrifices his own joy and self, *and his own sorrow too,* to help others – *if they truly need it!* And if his inmost voice tells him to.

And so, in this End-moment, Scimarajh, the seeker, for the very first time *understood Love, which forgets self.*

And Scimarajh surged anew for his helper; grabbed him like a dear treasure – *which he was; for to help him was Scimarajh final task –* and *turned Upwards* again.

And nature awoke with him!

The light encircled him, the power gripped him and pulled him upwards. And he began to hear the little whispering voices again!

Good! Oh, good, good man thou art, Scimarajh, who ever heedeth the inmost voice, and who has learned the art of forgetting self! The blessings of the Supreme Ruler abide with thee! Abide with thee forever and ever more...

The wild rush through the shinning portal sapped whatever little strength Scimarajh still had. He wanted air, air, air!

He came out of the light hearth, his helper still in his hands. The top of the lake spread but metres above. Hey! Were those fresh fishes he could see swimming around him in the lake? How come he had never seen them before? *What* was this lake?

Now it was left to his own strength again.
Oh Lord, endowest Thou me with fresh strength to Succeed!"

And a little energy seeped in. He started to swim upwards towards the surface of the lake, towards the bank. Tired. Oh, was he tired?!...

Don't stop! Go on! You can make it! – the little nature-workers whispered into his braveheart.

And then...

Ah! –

The surface!

His head broke through the surface and he gulped in the largest quantity of air he ever had at one moment in his life consumed.

It was dark outside. The sun had gone down. *Had he been in there so long?* A few stars dotted the sky, a full moon shone soft and mellow-bright over the world, like a greeting, a welcome-call, from Heaven up above.

But he did not permit himself to reflect over all this, or to swim in the euphoria of breathing again! He could not.

His helper! –

He hoisted his helper's body out of the lake and pushed him unto the bank. As he pushed him he himself also climbed out, shoving his helper further inland.

They both were there, dripping wet on the bank of the Lake of Love…

Scimarajh on his knees, his helper, flat on his back.

"Oh helper…helper!" Scimarajh called urgently in a hollow, tired voice and weakly shook the body of his helper, acting and speaking with as much energy as he could. Oh, he was tired…

He did not know what to do. He was loosing consciousness himself. The he saw the little elemental beings suddenly appear all around him and, closest to him, was their green-capped leader.

Oh, at last … at last…

His helping guide would have help.

But…but… - *his thinking was blurred, but he saw something he understood not! – why* were his little friends coming to *him* and not to his helper?

"No … no … not me," he tried to weakly say. "Help Helper. I'm okay. *He* needs it…" Fatigue covered his eyes as he searched the grass in front of him for his helper's body - …

It was gone. He was gone. Vanished. He, Scimarajh, was alone. In the twinkling of an eye … his "helper" had vanished and all that remained there where he had been was a little pool of water…or was it a pool of tears??

"But … but…" – but Scimarajh could talk no more. He was only dimly aware of the activity going on around him, of the fact that the grasses were brightening, aye, as he finally and finally and *finally* sank into a deep, deep slumber.

Scimarajh rested.

He had gone to the bottom of the Lake of Love and laboriously sought and fought for, freed and brought up what he discovered there:

Himself.

The wanderer was victorious.

Nature quietened again as Scimarajh slept the changing sleep.

The moon hid her face, the little elementals floated away. Let the bells prepare to ring. Yes.

Another human spirit has found himself, his home.

Che Chidi Chukwumerije

Epilogue:

REFLECTIONS

...

Che Chidi Chukwumerije

...

Andro-meh-dryadase, the green-capped leader of the littlers, looked up from his work and lifted his depthless eyes to the blue skies and remained in this posture for a few moments.

Then he dropped his tools, donned his green cap and sounded the call of the elementals through the woods.

They appeared from all sides a short while later.

"Scimarajh is awakened and refreshed and ready to approach the Shinning Gate of the Land of Bliss. He has accomplished his mission. He has found himself.

"Come; let us all go to him and give him a united final hearing and a deserving farewell, for his tenure here has been of benefit not only to himself but also to us.

"And our farewell shall also contain gratitude. And our gratitude shall find sight and sound, my fellow servants, as it should always be!"

And the little nature-workers followed Andro-meh-dryadase, their leader, in an orderly procession out of the woods and to the Lake of Love.

There they saw ... Scimarajh.

He had grown into a giant, almost twice his former size. He was dressed in a flowing white gown, brighter than snow, and from his eyes emanated a radiance probably never before seen by thine eyes, reader, nor mine.

Scimarajh stood on the bank of the Lake of Love and looked at himself.

He heard the nature-workers but he turned not, continued looking, seriousness residing peacefully upon his beautiful features.

The beings knew that he knew they were around. And they knew that *he* knew that they knew. For they knew that now he too could see and perceive, and understand, all our inner vibrations.

They arranged themselves noiselessly in a neat semi-circle and stood patiently waiting for him. He had become a wise one. He was communing for the last time with the Lake of Love because once he turned away from it again he would *never* turn back.

They knew this, so they left him to his deep thoughts and deep self-communion ... for they understand – yes *they* do!

The wind rustled the leaves and the wandering sojourner turned around.

Was this Scimarajh?

His countenance was suffused with peace, with love and with deliberation.

With firm and even, but gentle, strides he approached the little semi-circle of the little nature beings. In their centre and slightly forward stood Andro-meh-dryadase, their green-capped leader.

And gently, tenderly, but with so much controlled power, Scimarajh smiled...

And his smile was like the ascension of the sun. It spread warmth, and all the beings smiled back, ever so gentle, ever so true.

A moment of stillness... and then they all sat down.

"Andro-meh-dryadase..." said Scimarajh, his eyes resting upon the great little leader and then, roaming around:" Nature-workers ... hear ye the voice of one who hath found!"

Even the wind sat quietly, the birds nestled their lithe forms, nature listened:

"Life is a journey from immortality to immortality.

"Today I know this. Let no-one imagine that the Kingdom of Heaven is a place of rest. No. It is a place of the utmost height of activity. We do not live to die... nor wake up to slumber ... nay – we live to awaken into a more glorious day.

"Life is eternity-long. What is the point in being alive when one does not know the purpose for which one is alive?

"It is the duty of every creature to play a useful role in creation. To be able to do this, one must necessarily understand this creation and also one's self. One will then see therein the *Intention* of Him through and out of Whom the Creations arose!

If one does not know this, then one has to seek it. This is where the problem lies...

"A human child goes to school to learn how to fit into society. Thus also did the spirit-seed-germ journey from the Land of Bliss millennia into millennia ago in order to, through wandering, exploring, experiencing and learning, become capable of understanding the Will of Him through Whom the World also arose; and thereby to see the activity of Creation itself clearly and his own place therein.

"And Creation exists *only* for the joy of the creatures who live in it, who could only become conscious in an independently created realm *far* from the very *Fire* of God because such was *too hot!*

"And these creatures are you, I and all the many others. And we are of different types. And whereas some immediately come alive in their understanding and activity, or quickly and *faithfully* develop into it, like you ..., some others, like the members of my human race, need to go through a long, gradual process of slow development.

"But in the end the goal is the same.

"The perfection in the Land of Bliss was *still too high* for the spirit-germ. So he had to be taken far away ... beyond the Lake of Love, over the mountains of reflection and hope, behind the seven seas, beyond the seven forests, before the seven stark deserts ...

into that cool region known today as the world of men.

"We were meant to gradually and unitedly seek the Land of Bliss from there, and the experiences we would undergo in this process would mature and perfect us for the Land of Bliss. In the original plan, there was no issue of us *being purified of evil*...for already we were pure.

"Nor would the adventures have been harsh on us. Because, *then*, the seven deserts were not the stark-empty steaming dry earth that they today are. *Then* they were undulating plains where children could play, and the dried-up oases were lakes.

"And the seven hideous forests were not hideous forests, but great gardens full of angels, nature-workers and friendly animals, where youths could dream and form all their ideals and ideas, and remember the Land of Bliss.

"Nor were the seven roaring oceans the enemies of the wanderer which today they are. Mighty island-realms flourished there, amidst the oceans, as the points of the final perfecting of adult females and males. Here they could work and, in aligning themselves to the Supreme Will, the Will of God, beautify the world with magnificent works.

"And on approaching perfection here, they could move on over the mountains of reflection and hope, the emerald mountains which once those hard, rugged peaks were.

"Until the Lake of Love...

"Here is the point at which one should know one's self the most complete. The Lake of Love. Why is it called the Lake of Love? – twice did I ask this question and the only reply I received was that I should look in. And I saw myself.

"I did not understand. Now I do. I have the third time journeyed it, and down to the bottom; and have emerged alive ... and complete.

"The Lake of Love is the smallest obstacle facing the returning spirit and yet the greatest. It is here that one sheds *all, down to the tiniest of*, particles from the world without before proceeding into the Land of Bliss within.

"The Land of Bliss is no joke." Scimarajh's voice soared, his heart gushed, his serene eyes lifted. "The human spirit cannot wake up from sleep one day and then in an uninterested manner simply stagger half-cooked into It. Oh no! He has to *sojourn* ... he has to travel, has to change, has to go through *hard* inner experiences to atone for the thousands and thousands of years during which he has been *squandering the gift of life*. Indeed! *Man must repay...*

"After traversing all the worlds he must battle the Lake of Love. The Lake of Love is called so because it brings up before and within one *all* the buried faults and hidden weaknesses which one *must* overcome in order to get into the Land of Bliss.

"As long as one possesses even *one* little fault within one still, then one is yet to be perfect and thus will never be able to enter into the perfect kingdom. And no human being, on his own, will voluntarily seek out and address his faults, down to the slightest, most insignificant one. No human being can even *do* so anymore. He will still inevitably shield his inmost, most "harmless" ego away from the interrogative eye of his own self-conquering mission, and half-consciously skip over some "tiny" weaknesses which he has. *But no distortion or weakness is either harmless or tiny, none is truly insignificant.* The only difference between a seed and a tree...is time.

"And so it is *imperative* that a human being have his deepest, most hidden sins shown to him...those sins which he will never on his own acknowledge because they are *too intrinsic*, you see?

"And this is what the Lake of Love does. It faces the individual with his *final decision* that affects his life and time. It shows him his faults, his self. And not just shows it to him but arranges events before him in such a way that to overcome them he must conquer his faults, that is, face himself and be free.

"And that way he has only gained, and the Love of God the Father has saved him. *Hence, the name: Lake of Love.*

"Now I see. How difficult it is for a human soul to

traverse this last obstacle depends on how willingly he has been allowing all other previous experiences to show him his real self.

"If he has only gained half-the-lessons, then the Lake of Love will be a painful issue for him.

"And the Lake of Love *will be a painful* and troublesome issue for every human-being of today, just like it was for me, because now not only are we imperfect but – *even worse – we are impure!*

"And Life abhors, above all, impurity...

"The Lake of Love, now I know, is but my own self. For every human being, Lovelake forms himself into an expression of that very same person's true self, and challenges him to overcome his deepest weaknesses! And that is why it is so insurmountable, because the most difficult conquest for every conqueror is actually but his own self ... - and were he truly conquered of self, all desires to conquer others also would leave him.

"My own self. Everything clear. The first little turbulence in the upper part of the lake was my thoughts. The force represented my impetuous thoughts ... the chill represented my selfish thoughts...and the dizziness my confused thoughts.

"And in order to go through this realm I had to *stop such thinking, and relax, and heed the voices of my intuition and you*, faithful guardians of man the faithless wandering spirit.

"And that they were the first, least troublesome and uppermost obstacles signifies that our thoughts are the weakest of all our inner-movements, and the first to disturb us. Nevertheless they are dangerous and can destroy a person when he is always occupied with and only in them. Instead we must be always *intuitive*, even when we think.

"Next came the two portals. The shinning hearth and the black hole. They at first seem to be at the *floor of the lake*, and yet that is not the actual floor, which fact is proved by the *fact* that they are there, leading ... inside.

"This is to tell me that what I think is the deepest in me *is still not the deepest!* No man's true nature is both good and bad. There is something yet deeper ... – light and darkness cannot dwell together in the heart of man because this heart is originated from light and not from darkness.

"And so, if one sees both light and dark within him, one should investigate, indeed *one will finally be forced to journey*, that is to *experience* the dark side of himself in order to know *what* it is and *why* it is there where it should not be; that is, you must come to terms with yourself, must be confronted by all that is wrong in you, man must complete his fate! It will *catch* you –

"And that was why I was instructed by you, who knew all this already, to enter bravely into the inevitable black hole, that is, to accept my calling, self-formed, returned destiny. My fate. And *what did I see?* – the black hole was my fear and, in entering it, I conquered it. And found my heart.

"*Follow your heart!* Follow the light, not the dark! Follow the light bravely through even the darkest night ... I did. And found me; my heart.

"And in my heart I found *both good and bad-disguised-as-good* – these were my true back-pack and the false one. And what this meant was that even though I was seeking the Light I also still secretly cherished material things and vanities. And, in deciding in favour of my faithful back-pack, I defeated this weakness finally. And appropriately the false bag became a fleeing, dying snake. And I embraced my pure longing.

"And then...the monster with my face, and my helper. In the lake I did not know what this meant. Now I do. My guide, my helper, my guardian, he told me that everybody has a helper, and when I told him that I was nobody's helper, he told me to wait and see. And in helping "him", I evidenced my willingness, activated the innate urge to help, which sleeps in every human being, and have also become a helping spirit and thus gave to another that love which was done to me, as all of us must ever do! Although, in the end, it was myself that I helped, and my destiny that I guided to its end. –

"But what was my helper doing at the bottom of the lake or, rather, at the bottom of my heart? And why was a monster that bore my face strangling him?

"Simple.

"My helper's duty towards me was to see me safely through my battles in the Lake of Love. As such he was bound to me and speaking to me in my heart.

"But on my part there was another person inside me. This was my old ugly self. My selfish ego. It refused to die and, so long as I was not succeeding, it was tantamount to my monster strangling the helper in me, that is, the old evil in me was defeating the strength and advice which my helper had put into me.

"And so I had to see this sight in order to learn to understand this truth and to close this cycle, too. And I dropped my back-pack again in order to attack the monster.

"This means: I had to choose. Either I tried to resurface with this little touch-treasure or I forsook it for the larger, eternal treasure. And I did.

"The back-pack signified *the past* for me, but conquering the monster was *in the present* because my heart wanted that. That was why as soon as I moved towards the monster, the bag slipped out of my hand. And, also, later when I had saved my helper, my urge to retrieve my bag was overwhelmed by my need to save my helper.

"And how did I defeat the monster? I inserted the key into his heart *and turned it*! And the key was supposed to be the instrument with which I would open up for myself the Gate that barred my forward advance into the Land of Bliss. And, in the end, *it was...*

"You see: my deeper monster was the final accumulation of all those my little faults and weaknesses which formerly I had encountered one by one and it was *it* that barred my way because to get to the kingdom, pure perfection had to arise in me and suffuse me completely. But how could it do this when in my heart an angel and a devil were fighting.

"The monster had to go. The gate had to be opened! And it was. When I turned the key inside it I defeated it and it broke up into pieces and vanished. The rotten ego was overcome. Now only the spirit was left.

"And I grabbed hold of my helper, or rather the *simulation* of my helper, who was the symbol of my journey.

"You see, I set off initially from the lifeless world of men to *find me my heart!* At long last. And, in the deepest sense my helper signified my heart ... bravely fighting a battle against all the wrong in me, but losing *unless help came ... and help came!* But my heart was then weak and almost dead. It needed salvation.

"What this has taught me is that the human spirit has sunk so deeply low and cultivated evil so strongly that now this evil is more powerful than he himself, and except help comes from without, *and man seeks it and unites with it with All his energy*, we *will* be lost.

"People can no longer free themselves from their bondage by themselves because the binder is, curiously, their *own* intellect. My own intellect. The intellect of human beings is like a machine that seeks only after material benefit. As such, the exclusively intellectual is *baffled* by and seeks to 'correct' what he understands not, which is the spirit and the heart, that which can forsake material benefit in its striving after light.

"Because of this the world of men has sunk too deeply as we human beings ignore the often hard to interpret inner voice, the gentle urging of the spirit and conscience, and respond instead to the tune of the roary ambition of the *Intellect* alone.

"And thus once I had brought my own inner strength to bear against my *own selfish mind – the monster with my face –* and saved my heart with the flashing key...then I needed not this key anymore.

"But I did not know this. So when the key got knocked out of my hand I wanted to go for it. And, this time, for the first time, no warning voice sounded to caution me ... for I had to, with open eyes, decide which was more important: a used metal or my bleeding heart...

"And indeed I did.

"Even the leaving, *the shedding*, of my back-pack

containing my garments and jewels at the bottom of the Lake of Love has a deeper meaning. You don't enter Paradise with earthly or worldly material, but with the robe, the answers, of the victorious spirit! For everything lies already now in my heart, *and the Key to the Shinning Gate of the Land of Bliss lies ever at the very bottom of the Lake of Love...*

"That is why God's Son commanded us on earth to *love* our neighbour even as ourselves. But these are just brief explanations, and verily on could I go, aye, on and ever on, unthreading my story and its phases, and unveiling secrets about men and life...but my journey has come to its end – "

Scimarajh paused for a while, as his words melted into the currents that would carry their life back to the earth-plane, perhaps to stir another Scimarajh awake ... that very world where men had only laughed at him, mocked and ridiculed him, called him a lost dreamer and a fool, pronounced him mad. But now he had overcome the Lake of Love and, inspite of all, yet was praying for that same world of men. Because not every fool is a fool, I guess, or is every lunatic finally insane. Believe it or not, some dreamers know what they are doing; and dreams die hard.

And then he spoke, his upward-gazing eyes slowly redescending unto the faces of the littlers:

"Little beings of nature! Continue to serve the development of all life faithfully as you have done from the primeval beginnings. The human race has fallen and failed, but not you.

"From the deepest depth of my heart I thank you for your loving and faithful help and guidance without which I would *have surely failed*. I thank ye..." His voice trembled. His hands sought the pouches of his white robe and he extracted a little, twinkling jewel. He extended his hands towards Andro-meh-dryadase.

Andro-meh-dryadase's eyes widened. *Where* had this gem come from? *He* had never seen it or its type before.

Scimarajh smiled. He saw Andro-meh-dryadase's surprised heart.

"The man you see today, friend, is not the same you saw yesterday. So do not be surprised that I have grown twice my size or am robed in new substance. 'Tis not magic-nay....

"Today, brother mine, I, through the faithful, fateful overcoming of harsh experiences, am born anew."

The wild wind, excited, suddenly arose powerfully – *would it break?* – no ... it sighed gently and finally rested again, breathing softly. Scimarajh had captured them all. And Andro-meh-dryadase's slightly quivering hands reached for the jewel, the other beings bowed their heads in wonder and respect, and gratitude there was.

Silence reigned. Peace and love.

Then Andro-meh-dryadase spoke:

"Scimarajh. Son of the earth. Your tenure with the past is over. It is worthy of praise how you can sit down here so controlled and calm, talking to us, when in your heart the yearning for your home, the longing to bestride the luminous eternal gardens of Paradise, is unbounded! I salute you! You tell us that we have helped you and have taught you but, in truth my friend, the student has been as always the teacher, the master eternally the servant..."

Tears misted Scimarajh's eyes over.

Now it was the turn of the littlers to present a gift to him. Andro-meh-dryadase made a basic sign and seven female, exquisitely fair and luminous, elemental beings from whose shoulders fluttered wings, floated over to him, bearing a case. They smiled and yet smiled not. To Scimarajh these silent females seemed to be the masters over the populous males...

"This comes to you at Heaven's Command," spoke Andro-meh-dryadase softly. "It comes *back to thee!*"

The green-capped littler opened the case and extracted an object, the like of which Scimarajh had never once seen. It was shinning.

It had a strange effect on him. He asked not what it stood for. In his heart of hearts, without words, *he knew*; and never would this knowledge be put into words. For the cycle means an end; and the end surely the beginning...

He stored it deep inside his heart and made it his ... *forever.*

Suddenly he felt complete.

No words to say.

Everybody arose again. Without any words they all knew that the time to separate had come. Time to say Good-bye - - -

"Thank you for patiently listening to me speak to myself *all this time*", Scimarajh said softly, "for I know that I have told you nothing new ..."

"And thank you, Scimarajh, for thanking us," their little green-capped leader replied quite mysteriously. "But you have indeed told us something new...yes, you have, great one." –

The trees straightened, grasses danced, and joyfully climbed the sun higher in the blue sky.

A moment of endearing tenderness descended on this beautiful valley. They stood and looked at each other – Scimarajh, human being ... and the conscious nature-beings ... *Indeed, Unity conquereth all!*

Aye, it was a moment of endearing tenderness.

Tears sought the earth.

"Let us pray," said somebody or, perhaps, everybody.

Souls opened, hearts sought the heavens as Scimarajh opened his lips and solemnly declared:

"Oh Lord ... Father of all ... we humbly vow to serve Thee, and Thee Alone, in *all eternity*! – AMEN."

Silent lay the Lake of Love below Scimarajh, the tireless traveller, as he walked away from the Valley of Transformation and began to ascend that towering bright Hill of Truth, on top of which stands the never-changing, ever-changing, immortally growing, nagging Land of Bliss. He was silent. Very silent. When you have gone to the bottom of the heart of love, you become mostly silent. It is normal.

Bliss and rapture encaptured him, spirit, giant, as he mounted the sloping gradient. He did not once turn to look back. A Sojourner never looks back. - - -

Still he was clear aware of the little beings behind him, following his Ascent with their loving animistic eyes. A horse galloped briefly in the meadows, its neigh a song, and a ding-dong so merry was on high ... - the heart of Scimarajh burst with joy!! He had lived through the Valley in the blink of an eye.

Now he mounted the Hill. It was another Kingdom of its own, this Crystal-hill, another tale. Finally he passed through and approached his Home upon the hilltop...

As he neared the Shinning Gate it slowly began to open...

A golden radiance began to seep through. Blue. Openness. It encircled him and filled him with bliss, the bliss which is unimaginable.

And then he was there!

The Gate parted completely to reveal ... his helper, standing there with outstretched arms and a smile of the deepest Love and Joy shinning out of his face. *Thou hast conquered!*, was the message in the smile; *Welcome back!* –

He was of equal size with the Scimarajh, dressed in an identical garment and held a crown in his hand.

The guardian angels did then uncross their swords, the guide called Scimarajh by a name which no mortal must ever hear ... and Scimarajh did not hesitate for one moment. He answered the Call and stepped into the realm of yon golden lights, the land of distant Giants, and received solemnly the all golden crown of the pure eternal life which his helper, friend, teacher and guide simply placed upon his arising head.

Through!

With elemental force a gust of golden wind surged and swirled around the two spirits, Scimarajh and his friend who had once appeared to him as a helper, a guardian and a guide and whose name we shall for this moment understand to be Lovelake.

A choir began to sing, an orchestra commenced the playing of the most beautiful piece of music ever heard by Scimarajh. Solemn and eternal and full of immortal joy!

The angels rejoiced. Another human-spirit, another flame, another prodigal son hath returned Home.

- -

Yea ... for one last, brief time-beat, Scimarajh remembered everything again, his whole life, it flashed out in him, and then he put his heart by his brother's and together they turned and vanished, through the passing golden wind, into the *indescribable* Land of eternal Bliss, as the purity-silver First Gate of Paradise clicked shut again behind them, so to stay until yet another wanderer again came walking up this Hill one day. –

And below, in the beautiful valley, Andro-meh-dry-adase and the other faithful, strong nature-workers of Substantiality, this rare band of Littlers, slowly and noiselessly dispersed and went back to their Post; and when they were all gone, it was silent in the green Valley of Transformation ... and there in its heart peacefully waited again ... eternal ...

the Lake of Love.

The Lake of Love

Author's Note:
What is the Lake of Love?

...

"THE LAKE of Love" is not set in any recognisable place or time. It is just concepts that have arisen and taken on form. Actually it is more than just 'concepts'. It is actually very real and, for me, tangible. But, for some people, they may at first appear as 'philosophical concepts'. The theme is selfless love – not in terms of relationships or patriotism or filial love, i.e. not with focus upon any particular chosen recipient of it; but in terms of self-conquest and self-knowledge, thus with regards to the giver of it, and with the giver's struggle to become *such*: to stand in selfless love, able to direct it always and anytime there where it is needed.

I use as character a person called Scimarajh who

has journeyed far and wide in search of a place – or *state* – called the 'Land of Bliss'. He has overcome all manners of obstacles along the way, which I describe as seven deserts, seven forests and seven seas, until he sees (or intuitively senses) the Land of Bliss in the distance. But between himself and this state *stands* a quiet, still, tranquil lake. It is the lake of love, and will prove to be the most difficult hurdle to cross.

It thus turns out that the path to joy (the land of bliss) is love, but love is not love unless it be selfless. To be selfless, however, first one has to know one's self. The acquisition of this knowledge, in the reciprocal experiencing of one's self, is the most painful process a human being can go through.

This is the theme within the simple allegory called 'The Lake of Love'.

I wrote the story the Lake of Love in June of 1995. At that time I was strongly immersed in reflections about certain concepts which I linked with the attaining of adulthood. I had just gone through an intense personal tragedy some months earlier, and found myself often thinking about life and various aspects of it which seemed to me to be indetachable components of it. One of these subjects that continually occupied me inwardly was the concept of self-struggle, self-conquest, self-knowledge and self-realisation, as the different phases of one cycle.

The experiencing of the brevity of an earthlife, as well as of all the physical and psychological demands that it makes upon us, the question as to the meaning of it all, had gradually guided my thoughts to even more intense deliberations on this issue of self-purpose. Around this time I remembered a poem I had written some years earlier. It depicted in brief verses the inner struggles and thoughts of a man standing on the edge of a lake, about to dive in for a second time. He had gone in once and come up empty-handed. Then he had gone into the woods and strengthened himself. And now he was readying himself to go in a second and last time. And in he *had* to go because at the bottom of the lake lay the key to his happiness. Something like this went the poem.

I felt the urge to read this poem again, and searched through the madhouse of my books and notes and papers. It is very probable that if I had found it I would never have written this story. But I simply could not find it. So I decided to try and rewrite it. I immersed myself anew into the pictures, and then I asked myself how this man came to this lake at all in the first place and what kind of lake that was. Then, gradually, I discerned a man standing on a plateau, gazing yearningly across to a hilltop on the other side of the valley. In the man's eyes I saw a long struggle behind him. And then as he descended the plateau, nature spoke to him. Until he, in the valley, suddenly found his path blocked by a lake, a lake that would be impassable until he had conquered his own self. It suddenly became clear to me that such a lake could only be Love. And thus was the theme at once clear in my mind.

As I stood before the thought and gazed at the idea to write the lake of love, as a story this time and not a poem, an urge I now felt quite powerfully within me, I had to decide what kind of story it would be.

Finally I decided to write it in absolutes, almost like the notebook to an adult fairy-tale, because only so could I directly address the core concepts that I was trying to work out for myself in my mind. I gave the concepts form and put them into motion, and then observed how they played out in my story. So the writing of it became essentially for me a personal study, an attempt to bring together a group of thoughts into an ordered and meaningful picture with a message. The thoughts were not already clearly ordered in my mind before I wrote it, but the process of writing it ordered them out for me. Each time I got stuck in my unravelling of a concept, the whole story came to a halt too, because every event in the story is a living concept put into form. The story is simply a moving through a series of concepts. And thus, writing the Lake of Love became for me also almost like a personal struggling with a lake of love.

I wrote it as an advice to myself. A recognising and

acknowledging to myself of the heights and simple absolutes in which true ideals are embodied, as we struggle with ourselves and our shortcomings. The choice to strive after them is left to each person. But they will always be there, unchangeable and incorruptible, the inner gates to true humanity.

And blocking the path to this gate will always be a lake of love.

www.ingramcontent.com/pod-product-compliance
Lightning Source LLC
Chambersburg PA
CBHW020252150626
46552CB00020B/784